FROM MYTHS TO MINDSETS

TIMELESS LESSONS FOR TODAY'S CHALLENGES

DEEPAK SHARMA

Contents

Contents

Preface

Throughout history, mythology has served as a mirror to humanity's deepest aspirations, fears, and questions. It is in these timeless tales—of heroes and villains, of gods and mortals—that we find reflections of our own struggles and triumphs. Yet, in a world defined by speed, technology, and constant change, we often overlook the wisdom embedded in these ancient narratives.

This book is an attempt to bridge that gap. From Myths to Mindsets is not just a journey through mythology but an exploration of how these age-old stories hold powerful lessons for navigating the complexities of modern life. From questions of leadership and ethics to the pursuit of purpose and balance, these themes resonate as deeply today as they did centuries ago.

At the heart of this narrative is Ananya, an individual like many of us—searching for clarity, grappling with uncertainties, and striving to find meaning in her choices. Through her journey, we meet mentors, explore dilemmas, and uncover the profound intersections between ancient wisdom and modern challenges.

This book does not claim to provide all the answers. Instead, it invites you to reflect, to question, and perhaps, to rediscover the power of stories you thought you already knew. The lessons of mythology are not confined to history books or temples—they are alive, waiting to be reimagined and applied in your everyday life.

As you turn these pages, I encourage you to step into Ananya's shoes, engage with her reflections, and draw your own parallels. After all, the journey from myths to mindsets is not just hers—it is one we all must undertake to grow, lead, and live meaningfully.

Welcome to a narrative of transformation, where the past meets the present and wisdom becomes action.

Let the journey begin.

With gratitude,
Deepak Sharma

Acknowledgements

Writing From Myths to Mindsets has been a journey of introspection, discovery, and immense learning. This book would not have been possible without the contributions, guidance, and support of countless individuals who have inspired, encouraged, and challenged me along the way.

To my readers, you are the heart of this work. Your curiosity and openness to new perspectives give meaning to these pages. This book is as much yours as it is mine, and I hope it serves as a bridge between timeless wisdom and the challenges of our modern lives.

To the stories of mythology—timeless, profound, and ever-relevant—thank you for being a guiding light. The lessons you hold continue to inspire and remind us of that answers to today's questions often lie in the past.

To those who mentored me, both directly and indirectly, your insights, patience, and belief in this project have shaped its every chapter. Your wisdom mirrors the mentors in this book, and your encouragement has been my strength.

To my family and friends, thank you for your unwavering support and understanding throughout this journey. Your faith in me has been a constant source of motivation.

Lastly, to all the unnamed heroes in my life—your silent acts of kindness, your thoughtful conversations, and your presence have left an indelible mark. This book is, in many ways, a reflection of the impact you've had on me.

As I conclude this chapter of my journey, I remain humbled by the collective contributions that have brought this book to life. To each

of you, my deepest gratitude.
This is for all of us who continue to search, reflect, and grow.

With love and gratitude,
Deepak Sharma

Disclaimer

From Myths to Mindsets: Timeless Lessons for Today's Challenges is a work of creative nonfiction that blends insights from mythology with modern-day contexts to provide thought-provoking perspectives on personal and professional growth.

While this book draws from mythological stories, interpretations and conclusions presented here are the author's own and do not claim to represent any definitive religious, cultural, or scholarly views. The intent is not to promote or favour any particular belief system but to explore universal lessons and their relevance to modern challenges.

The characters, scenarios, and reflections in this book, although inspired by myths, have been crafted to foster introspection and learning. Any resemblance to real individuals, living or deceased, is purely coincidental and unintentional.

Readers are encouraged to engage with this book as a tool for inspiration and reflection rather than a substitute for professional or expert advice in personal, professional, or spiritual matters.

The author and publisher disclaim any liability arising from the use or interpretation of the content within these pages. The ultimate goal is to spark curiosity, promote dialogue, and encourage readers to explore their own journey of understanding and growth.

Segment 1 - Rediscovering Ancient Wisdom

"*The stories we inherit are more than echoes—they are compasses, waiting to guide us through the chaos of now.*"

CHAPTER ONE

WHY MYTHS MATTER

The Veil of the Familiar

It was a quiet evening when Ananya found herself staring at the framed painting in her grandfather's study. A familiar scene—a hero holding a bow, a chariot nearby, and a celestial figure whispering words of wisdom. She had seen this painting countless times growing up, yet something about it struck her differently that day.

"What's the story behind this?" she asked, hoping for a quick explanation.

Her grandfather smiled, setting his book aside. "It's not just a story, my dear. It's a question—one that's as relevant today as it was centuries ago."

That night, Ananya wasn't given an answer. Instead, she was left with the story of Arjuna on the battlefield, hesitant to act, torn between duty and morality. As she tried to fall asleep, one thought kept returning: Why does it feel like I've stood on that battlefield too?

The Echoes of Ancient Voices

What is it about myths that continue to haunt us, even in a world dominated by science and progress? Perhaps it's because myths are more than mere stories.

They are mirrors, showing us not just who we were but who we are and might become.

The myths of the past don't die; they adapt. They find their way into boardroom dilemmas, late-night doubts, and whispered confessions. When we question whether to chase ambition or choose contentment, we are echoing Icarus's flight too close to the sun. When we wonder whether to take a stand or stay silent, we are reliving Arjuna's pause on the battlefield.

A Conversation with Time

Consider this: myths don't lecture—they invite us into dialogue. They don't tell us what to think; they show us how to think. The beauty of mythology lies in its ambiguity. Every character, every choice, every consequence holds multiple truths.

The tale of the phoenix, for instance, isn't just about rebirth—it's about the courage to endure the fire. When we face loss or failure, the myth doesn't offer a solution, but it does whisper: You're not alone in this. Others have walked this path too.

Today's Questions, Yesterday's Stories

Ananya's experience isn't unique. Each of us, in our moments of uncertainty or despair, reaches for a story—something to make sense of the chaos. And myths, with their timeless themes, offer clarity:

- Who am I?
- What should I do?
- Why does this matter?

What separates myths from other narratives is their universality. A farmer in a small Indian village and a tech entrepreneur in Silicon Valley may never meet, but they both understand the longing for purpose, the burden of responsibility, and the weight of choices.

The Mythical Lens

Imagine viewing your life through the lens of mythology. What if your challenges weren't random obstacles but part of a larger story? What if your fears weren't weaknesses but the shadows of dragons yet to be slain?

This isn't to romanticize hardship but to reframe it. Myths remind us that life's trials aren't punishments—they're invitations. Invitations to grow, to reflect, and to transform.

Ananya couldn't sleep that night. She kept thinking about the battlefield, the hesitation, and the choices that defined Arjuna. The next morning, she didn't wake up with answers.

But she did wake up with a different question:

What battle am I standing on the edge of?

And perhaps, that's where all stories begin—not with certainty, but with curiosity.

CHAPTER TWO

THE UNIVERSAL THREADS OF MYTHOLOGY

The Unlikely Map

Ananya found herself in a bustling café that evening, sipping her coffee as the city hummed around her. Across the table sat Rehan, an old friend from college, now a cultural historian. They hadn't met in years, but as she shared her recent obsession with myths, Rehan leaned back with an amused smile.

"Do you know what's fascinating about mythology?" he asked, pulling a worn map out of his bag. "Every culture, every corner of the world, tells the same stories—just with different accents."

He unfolded the map, not of countries but of myths. On it were lines connecting Persephone's descent into the underworld to the Indian story of Sita's captivity in Lanka. Another traced the Greek hero Odysseus's wanderings to the Nordic saga of Sigurd.

"Think about it," Rehan said. "Why does every culture, no matter how isolated, tell tales of love, betrayal, redemption, and courage?

It's as if humanity has always been trying to decode the same puzzle."

The Shared DNA of Stories

Ananya studied the map, her coffee forgotten. "So, it's not just a coincidence?" she asked.

"It's not," Rehan replied. "Think of it as the shared DNA of humanity. Myths aren't just stories—they're survival guides. They emerged from the need to understand the world, to make sense of suffering, to inspire hope. And the best part? They've always been about us."

Ananya was intrigued. She leaned forward as Rehan explained the parallels:

- The flood myth, from Noah's Ark in the Bible to Manu's tale in Indian texts, reflecting humanity's fear of nature's wrath and the hope for renewal.
- The trickster archetype—be it Loki in Norse myths or Krishna's playful wisdom—revealing the value of wit and unpredictability.
- The hero's journey, universal yet personal, a metaphor for every individual's quest for meaning.

A Bridge Across Cultures

Later that night, Ananya found herself thinking about how similar we all are, despite the borders and languages that separate us. It was comforting, in a way, to know that the questions she struggled with were not hers alone.

As she pondered, she remembered a story her grandmother used to tell—a tale of Savitri, the woman who outwitted the god of death to save her husband. She smiled, realizing the story wasn't so different from Orpheus's journey to rescue Eurydice. Both were about love, courage, and the fight against inevitability.

Rehan had been right. The lines connecting these myths weren't just on a map; they were etched in human hearts.

The Myth Beneath the Surface

Ananya couldn't help but wonder: If these myths were so universal, what else could they teach her about life?

She thought of her own challenges—moments of doubt, relationships that felt frayed, ambitions that seemed just out of reach. Could these ancient stories, passed down through generations, hold the answers she was looking for?

Perhaps myths weren't just reflections of humanity's past but tools for navigating its present.

The next day, Ananya called Rehan. "I want to know more," she said, her voice steady. "But not just the stories. I want to understand how they fit into the lives we live today."

Rehan laughed. "You're starting to see the threads, aren't you? Let's untangle them together."

As she hung up, Ananya realized something profound. The myths weren't just about gods and heroes. They were about her, too. And she was just beginning to unravel their secrets.

CHAPTER THREE

THE LENS OF MODERNITY

The Noise of Now

Ananya was stuck in traffic, the blaring horns of impatient drivers and the hum of city life pressing against her thoughts. Her mind drifted to the conversation she had with Rehan. He had promised to meet her again, this time with stories that were supposed to "redefine how she saw the world."

"Stories," she muttered under her breath. "How can stories compete with algorithms, data, and the pace of now?"

But the thought lingered. As she watched the chaos unfold outside her window, it occurred to her: wasn't today's world its own kind of myth? A story being written by millions every day, yet so many of its characters—like her—felt lost in the narrative.

Finding the Myth in the Modern

Rehan arrived late that evening, carrying a stack of books and an unshakable grin. "I have a challenge for you," he said as he sat across from her. "Find the myth in your day."

"My day?" she asked, perplexed.

"Yes. In the traffic, the meetings, the decisions you made. Myths aren't just in old texts—they're living, breathing parts of our world."

He opened one of the books and began to read aloud:

- *The story of Prometheus stealing fire from the gods to give humanity knowledge.*
- *The tale of Saraswati, the goddess of wisdom, inspiring creativity, and clarity.*
- *The trickster Loki, stirring chaos to reveal hidden truths.*

Ananya listened, her scepticism melting away. "So, you're saying myths are metaphors?"

"More than that," Rehan replied. "They're lenses. They help us see patterns, understand conflicts, and make sense of what feels overwhelming. The characters in these myths? They're archetypes we meet every day—in ourselves and others."

The Archetypes Among Us
Over the next few days, Ananya began to notice the myths woven into her life.

- *Her ambitious colleague, who refused to compromise on his dreams, reminded her of Icarus—daring but precarious.*
- *Her own hesitation to take on a leadership role echoed Arjuna's indecision on the battlefield.*
- *A mentor who guided her through a tough decision felt like the wise Athena, offering counsel in times of uncertainty.*
- *Rehan had been right. The stories weren't relics—they were everywhere, shaping how she perceived herself and the people around her.*

A New Perspective

One evening, as Ananya prepared a presentation for work, she found herself struggling with how to frame her ideas. She thought of Prometheus again—the defiant act of stealing fire not just as rebellion but as an act of service.

She paused, her pen hovering over the page. Maybe her ideas didn't need to be perfect. Maybe they just needed to ignite something in the people who heard them.

The Mirror of Mythology

That night, Ananya called Rehan. "Do you think these myths were written with us in mind?"

Rehan laughed. "Not us, specifically. But they were written for humans, by humans. And we haven't changed as much as we think we have."

"Then why does it feel like they're speaking directly to me?"

"Because they are. Myths are mirrors—they reflect back the questions we're too afraid to ask ourselves."

As Ananya hung up, she looked around her small apartment. The myths she had once dismissed as irrelevant now seemed to glow with new meaning. She opened her laptop, a bold thought taking shape in her mind: If myths are lenses, how can I use them to see my life more clearly?

And with that, she began to write—not a story, but questions. Questions that could only be answered by living the myth she was just beginning to discover.

THE HERO WITHIN

The Weight of Expectations

Ananya's days had begun to feel like a series of ticking clocks. Meetings, deadlines, and social obligations piled on her shoulders, each demanding her attention. That evening, as she stood on her apartment balcony, staring at the sprawling city below, she felt the familiar ache of inadequacy.

"Why does it feel like I'm always falling short?" she thought aloud.

It wasn't just her own expectations—it was the weight of others' beliefs in her potential. The silent nods in meetings, the casual "you'll figure it out" from friends, and the unspoken assumption that she was always capable.

As she sank into the solitude of her thoughts, her phone buzzed. It was Rehan. "Tomorrow. Noon. The park," his message read.

The Call to Adventure

The next day, Ananya found Rehan sitting on a bench, a book in hand. He didn't greet her immediately. Instead, he opened the book and began to read:

"When the young prince Rama was exiled to the forest, he didn't ask, 'Why me?' He didn't question the injustice of it. Instead, he accepted his fate and embarked on a journey that would define him—not as a victim, but as a hero."

Rehan closed the book and looked at her. "Does this sound familiar?"

Ananya frowned. "Are you saying I'm like Rama?"

"I'm saying everyone is, at some point," Rehan replied. "The story of the hero isn't about being extraordinary—it's about answering the call. Even when it's unfair. Especially when it's unfair."

The Journey of the Hero

Rehan began to sketch a pattern in the dirt with a stick, drawing a simple circle. "This is the Hero's Journey," he said. "Every myth, every great story, follows this path. But here's the thing—they aren't just stories. They're maps for us to follow."

Ananya watched as he divided the circle into segments:

1. The Call to Adventure: A challenge or opportunity disrupts the hero's ordinary life.
2. The Threshold: The hero steps into the unknown, leaving behind comfort and certainty.
3. The Ordeal: A test that pushes the hero to their limits, revealing hidden strengths.
4. The Return: The hero comes back transformed, carrying lessons for the world.

A Modern Parallel

"You're standing at the threshold," Rehan said, meeting her gaze. "But you're hesitating."

Ananya felt the truth of his words. "Because I'm scared," she admitted. "What if I'm not enough?"

Rehan leaned back, his expression thoughtful. "You know, Arjuna asked Krishna the same thing. He looked at the battlefield, at the people he loved standing on both sides, and said, 'I can't do this.' But Krishna didn't tell him to be fearless. He told him to act with faith—to trust the process, even when the outcome was unclear."

The Hero in Indian Mythology

Rehan's words stirred something deep within Ananya. She had always admired heroes like Rama and Arjuna, but she had never seen herself in their stories. They were divine, extraordinary. How could their journeys apply to her, an ordinary woman navigating the chaos of modern life?

Rehan seemed to read her mind. "The beauty of Indian mythology," he said, "is that it doesn't separate the divinefrom the human. Rama was a prince, yes, but his struggles were deeply human—loss, exile, the weight of responsibility. And Arjuna's doubts? They're your doubts, too. That's the point of these stories. They're not about perfection; they're about perseverance."

Answering the Call

As the sun began to set, Rehan stood and offered Ananya his hand. "The question isn't whether you're ready," he said. "It's whether you're willing."

Ananya hesitated for a moment, then took his hand. She wasn't sure what lay ahead, but for the first time in weeks, she felt a spark of clarity.

That night, as she sat down to plan her week, she found herself thinking not about tasks but about thresholds. She made a list—not of goals, but of fears. And for each fear, she wrote a single question: What would Rama or Arjuna do?

It wasn't a perfect strategy, but it was a start.

The following morning, Ananya woke up earlier than usual. She stood at the edge of her balcony, the city still draped in the soft hues of dawn.

For the first time in a long while, she didn't feel weighed down.

She didn't have answers yet. But she had a direction. And maybe, just maybe, that was enough to begin.

CHAPTER FIVE

THE UNSEEN ALLIES

The Web of Support

Ananya was in her office, staring at a blank document on her laptop. The cursor blinked impatiently, as if mocking her hesitation. She had promised her team a strategy presentation, but the ideas felt scattered, her confidence elusive.

Her phone vibrated, snapping her out of her thoughts. It was a message from her father: "Never forget—Hanuman didn't know his own strength until he was reminded of it. Perhaps, you just need to be reminded too."

She smiled, though the weight of doubt still lingered. Could her father's words hold the key to her struggle?

Hanuman and the Mountain

That evening, Ananya met Rehan at their usual café. Over cups of steaming chai, she recounted her father's message.

Rehan's eyes lit up. "Ah, the story of Hanuman retrieving the Sanjeevani herb. Do you know why that tale is so powerful?"

Ananya shook her head, curious.

"Hanuman didn't realize the extent of his powers until Jambavan reminded him," Rehan began. "He had forgotten his divine strength because of a curse. But once reminded, he leaped across mountains and oceans, lifted a mountain, and brought it back to save Lakshman. That's what makes him relatable—his journey isn't just about physical strength, but the realization of inner potential."

Mentors and Catalysts

"Think about it," Rehan continued. "We're all like Hanuman at some point. We doubt ourselves, even when we have the abilities within us. And often, it takes someone else—our own Jambavan—to help us see our potential."

Ananya pondered his words. She thought of the people in her life—mentors, friends, and even colleagues—who had nudged her forward when she faltered.

"But what about those who don't have a Jambavan?" she asked.

"They do," Rehan replied. "Sometimes, it's a book, a memory, or even an inner voice. The trick is to recognize it."

The Mahabharata's Lesson on Allies

Rehan leaned forward. "And it's not just about recognizing your strength—it's about understanding your allies. Take the Mahabharata. The Pandavas didn't win the war alone.

They had Krishna as their guide, Draupadi as their anchor, and Bhima as their powerhouse. Every victory, every challenge they overcame, was a collective effort."

Ananya nodded, remembering how Krishna's wisdom had often

tipped the scales in favour of the Pandavas.

"But what about Karna?" she asked. "He was just as capable, yet he lost."

"Exactly," Rehan said. "Karna's story is a reminder that even the strongest individuals need the right support. His loyalty to Duryodhana was admirable, but it came at the cost of his own growth. In contrast, the Pandavas embraced their allies and shared their burdens. That's why their journey resonates—it's a story of collaboration, not isolation."

Applying the Lessons

The next day, Ananya returned to her office with a new perspective. She called a team meeting, something she rarely did.

"I've been working on the strategy presentation," she began, "but I think it'll be stronger if we approach it together."

Her team exchanged surprised glances but quickly dived into brainstorming. By the end of the day, the once-daunting task felt lighter, even energizing. Ananya realized that her father and Rehan had been right— strength wasn't just about what she could do alone, it was about the support she could embrace.

That evening, as Ananya walked home, she thought of Hanuman and Jambavan, Krishna and the Pandavas, and the allies in her own life. She felt a newfound gratitude for the web of support around her—a reminder that, like the heroes of mythology, she didn't have to navigate her challenges alone.

For the first time, the weight on her shoulders felt less like a burden and more like an opportunity.

And she knew she was ready to leap, just as Hanuman had, trusting the strength within and the allies beside her.

THE STRENGTH IN STILLNESS

The boardroom was abuzz with chatter as Ananya prepared to present her team's latest project. She adjusted the projector settings, her heart pounding slightly louder than usual. The stakes were high—this presentation could determine the trajectory of a critical campaign.

As she stood at the podium, her mind drifted briefly to a conversation she had with Rehan a few weeks earlier. He had spoken of a moment in mythology that had stayed with her since.

The Stillness Before the Storm

Rehan had recounted a scene from the Mahabharata. It wasn't one of the grand battles or Krishna's eloquent teachings but rather a quieter, overlooked moment.

"Do you remember when Draupadi was humiliated in court?" he asked.

Ananya nodded. Everyone knew that story—the dice game, the disrobing, and Krishna's divine intervention.

"But do you know what stood out to me?" Rehan continued. "It wasn't the rage of the Pandavas or the cruelty of the Kauravas. It was Draupadi's stillness.

Amid the chaos, when everyone was shouting and scheming, she stood rooted in her dignity. That stillness was her strength. It wasn't passive—it was powerful."

The Power of Poise

As Ananya clicked through her presentation slides, she thought of Draupadi's stillness. It wasn't an absence of emotion, but a deliberate pause—a moment to anchor oneself before responding.

She had faced her own share of turmoil recently. A series of setbacks at work had left her questioning her abilities. Yet, through Rehan's mentorship and her growing understanding of mythological parallels, she had come to realize the importance of grounding herself in the face of adversity.

The Modern Parallel

"Think about it," Rehan had said during their discussion. "In a world that demands instant reactions—emails, notifications, meetings—stillness is almost revolutionary. It's not about inaction; it's about choosing your action wisely."

He had shared another story, this time from the Ramayana. When Sita was abducted and imprisoned in Lanka, she refused to bow to despair. She waited, patient but determined, her resolve unbroken. That stillness wasn't submission; it was quiet defiance.

Ananya's Decision

As the Q&A session began, a senior executive questioned the

viability of her proposal. The words stung, but Ananya resisted the urge to defend herself immediately. Instead, she paused, taking a deep breath.

In that moment of stillness, she saw the bigger picture. The question wasn't an attack; it was an opportunity to clarify and strengthen her case.

"Thank you for raising that point," she said, her voice steady. "Let me elaborate on how we've accounted for that risk."

Her response was met with nods of approval. For the first time, Ananya felt the power of stillness—of pausing not out of fear, but out of strength.

Reflections

Later that evening, as she walked home, Ananya replayed the events of the day. She realized that stillness wasn't just a pause; it was a choice. It was the space between reaction and response, where clarity emerged.

She thought of Draupadi and Sita, of their quiet yet formidable strength.

In their stories, she found a blueprint—not for inaction, but for deliberate, thoughtful action.

In the stillness of the night, Ananya sat on her balcony, looking at the city lights. She felt a deep sense of gratitude for the ancient stories that had begun to shape her modern journey.

Strength, she realized, wasn't always about moving forward. Sometimes, it was about standing still rooted, deliberate, and unshaken.

CHAPTER SEVEN

THE WEIGHT OF CHOICES

Ananya stood at the crossroads of her career—two opportunities lay before her, each promising a vastly different future. One was a promotion within her current organization, offering stability but little excitement. The other was a role at a startup, brimming with possibilities but fraught with uncertainty.

The decision had been haunting her for days. Every time she thought she had made up her mind, a new doubt emerged. The weight of the choice felt unbearable.

The Dilemmas of Heroes

That evening, she found herself at Rehan's office again, seeking his perspective.

"Rehan, have you ever felt completely torn between two options, where neither feels entirely right or wrong?" she asked, her voice heavy with frustration.

Rehan smiled knowingly. "Let me tell you about someone who faced a similar dilemma—Karna."

Ananya sat up, intrigued.

Karna's Struggle

Rehan began, "Karna was one of the most skilled and valorous warriors of the Mahabharata, but his life was defined by one relentless conflict: loyalty versus righteousness. Born a Kshatriya but raised as a charioteer's son, he struggled with identity and acceptance. When Duryodhana offered him friendship and status, Karna's gratitude bound him to the Kauravas prince.

"But then came the Kurukshetra war," Rehan continued, "where Karna had to choose between his loyalty to Duryodhana and his own conscience. He knew that supporting Duryodhana meant standing on the side of adharma, yet he couldn't bring himself to betray the man who had given him dignity. His choice, though loyal, cost him his life and legacy."

The Modern Mirror

Ananya leaned back, her mind racing. "So, you're saying it's about weighing the cost of our choices?"

"Exactly," Rehan said. "Every choice has a cost, Ananya. The key is to understand what you're willing to pay for and why. Karna chose loyalty, but it came at the expense of his own moral compass. What about you? What do you value most—stability or growth?"

Ananya sighed. "Both have their merits. But how do I decide?"

The Framework of Dharma

Rehan leaned forward. "Let's look at it through the lens of dharma. Dharma isn't a set of rigid rules; it's about aligning your actions with your purpose and values. When Arjuna hesitated on the battlefield,

Krishna reminded him of his dharma—not as a warrior, but as someone responsible for restoring justice. It's not always easy, but clarity comes when you focus on your core principles."

He paused, then added, "And remember, no choice is perfect. What matters is making peace with the one you make."

Ananya's Epiphany

The next morning, Ananya went for a run, her mind still churning over their conversation. As she jogged through the park, she realized something profound: her dilemma wasn't just about the roles; it was about her fears.

She was afraid of failure at the startup and afraid of stagnation at her current job. But both fears stemmed from the same place—an uncertainty about her own capabilities.

She stopped running and sat on a bench, catching her breath. It wasn't the opportunities that needed clarity; itwas her own sense of direction. What did she truly want? What aligned with her dharma?

The Decision

Back at her desk later that week, Ananya drafted her resignation letter. She had chosen the startup. It wasn't the safer option, but it resonated with her desire for growth and purpose.As she pressed "Send," a sense of relief washed over her. The weight of the decision had lifted—not because it was easy, but because it felt right.

Reflections

That evening, Ananya called Rehan. "I made my choice," she said.

"And?" Rehan asked.

"It feels like jumping into the deep end of the pool," she admitted. "But for the first time, I'm not afraid of the water."

Rehan chuckled. "Good. Remember, Ananya, it's not about avoiding dilemmas.

It's about learning from them. Even Karna, with all his struggles, left us with a lesson—sometimes, the hardest choices shape the strongest characters."

As Ananya hung up, she looked at her reflection in the mirror. The person staring back wasn't someone weighed down by indecision anymore. She was someone who had embraced the power—and the price—of choice.

Segment 2 - Aligning Actions with Purpose

"In the realm of choices and chaos, clarity of intention is the compass that guides us to purpose."

CHAPTER EIGHT

THE ECHO OF INTENTIONS

The café buzzed with quiet conversations, the soft hum of coffee machines blending with the faint clinking of cups. Ananya sat at a corner table, her laptop open but untouched. She had spent the last hour staring at the same line of an email draft.

The new job at the startup had been everything she had expected—fast-paced, innovative, and incredibly demanding. Yet, something felt off. Despite her best efforts, her team's latest project wasn't aligning with the company's vision. The more she tried to steer it back on track, the more it seemed to drift.

"Lost in thought, or just hiding from the chaos?" a warm voice interrupted her reverie.

She looked up to see a man in his late 40s, his presence calm yet commanding. He had a slight smile and the kind of demeanour that instantly put people at ease.

"Maybe a bit of both," Ananya replied hesitantly, unsure how to react to the stranger's friendly tone.

"Mind if I join you? Looks like you could use a break," he said, gesturing to the empty chair across from her.

The New Mentor

Over the next hour, Ananya learned that the man's name was Sameer, a seasoned strategist with years of experience guiding organizations through transformations. Unlike Rehan, whose wisdom often came from stories and abstract ideas, Sameer had a more pragmatic, hands-on approach.

"Every problem," Sameer said, "is rooted in intent. What you're trying to achieve and why. If those aren't clear, no amount of effort will lead you to the right outcome."

His words struck a chord. Ananya had been so focused on executing the project that she hadn't paused to examine its core intentions.

The Mythological Parallel

As they spoke, Sameer shared a story that surprised her.

"Do you know the tale of Kaikeyi from the Ramayana?" he asked.

Ananya nodded. "She's the one who asked for Lord Rama's exile, right?"

"Exactly," Sameer said. "But do you know why she did it?"

"Wasn't it because of her ambition for her son Bharata?"

"That's the common interpretation," Sameer replied. "But if you look deeper, you'll see Kaikeyi was influenced by her maid, Manthara. Her intentions were unclear torn between love for her son and the fear of losing status. That confusion led to actions that disrupted an entire kingdom."

He paused, letting the weight of his words sink in. "Intentions are like the roots of a tree. If they're twisted or weak, the entire structure above will falter."

Ananya's Reflection

That night, Ananya revisited the project documents, this time with a different perspective. She began asking questions: Why were they pursuing this approach? What was the ultimate goal? And most importantly, did her team understand and share that vision?

As she worked, she realized that the project wasn't failing because of poor execution—it was failing because the intentions weren't aligned. The team was working hard, but without a unified purpose, their efforts lacked direction.

Realigning the Roots

The next day, Ananya called for an impromptu team meeting.

"I want us to step back for a moment," she began. "Before we go any further, let's revisit why we're doing this project.
What are we trying to achieve, and how does it connect to our larger goals?"

The room fell silent as her team processed her words. Slowly, they began to share their thoughts. Some admitted they weren't clear on the objectives, while others raised concerns about conflicting priorities.

By the end of the session, they had a clearer, more focused direction. Ananya felt a renewed sense of energy in the room—a collective understanding that had been missing before.

Lessons in Clarity

Later that evening, Sameer called to check in.

"How did it go?" he asked.

"Better than I expected," Ananya replied. "It wasn't easy, but I think we're finally on the same page."

"Good," Sameer said. "Remember, clarity of intention isn't just about what you do; it's about how you communicate it. When your actions align with your intentions, they create an echo—one that others can feel and follow."

As Ananya ended the call, she felt a sense of calm she hadn't experienced in weeks. The pressure was still there, but it no longer felt overwhelming.

She thought of Kaikeyi and the unintended consequences of unclear intentions. And she thought of Sameer's advice, which had guided her back to the roots of her work.

In the quiet of her room, Ananya made a promise to herself: no matter how chaotic things became, she would always take a moment to align her actions with her intentions.

Because, as Sameer had said, every action is an echo of its intent—and the strength of that echo can shape everything it touches.

CHAPTER NINE

THE WEB OF COLLABORATION

Ananya stood at the whiteboard, marker in hand, as her team gathered in the conference room. The energy in the room was palpably different from the last meeting. Aligning on their intentions had brought a sense of focus but now came the harder part—execution.

"Our goal is clear," Ananya began, pointing to the project's central objective written boldly at the top of the board. "But achieving it will require more than individual brilliance. It will require us to function as a team, as one cohesive unit."

Despite her words, she could sense hesitation in some faces. The idea of interdependence felt daunting to a group that had operated in silos for years.

The Mythological Parallel

Later that evening, Ananya sought Sameer's advice. She explained the situation, detailing how difficult it was to foster collaboration in a team conditioned to prioritize individual results.

Sameer listened patiently and then shared a story from the

Mahabharata.

"Have you heard of the story of the Pandavas and the construction of their palace in Indraprastha?" he asked.

Ananya nodded vaguely. "You mean the one where Duryodhana was tricked by the illusions in the palace?"

"Yes, but there's more to it than that," Sameer said. "The palace was a marvel of engineering and artistry, built with the combined efforts of the Pandavas and their allies. Bhima's strength laid the foundation, Arjuna's skill secured the structure, Yudhishthira's wisdom ensured it aligned with dharma, and Nakula and Sahadeva brought beauty and order to its design. Each contribution was unique, yet the result was seamless."

He paused, letting the thought settle. "That palace wasn't just a physical structure; it was a symbol of what can be achieved when individual strengths are woven together with a common purpose."

The Modern Challenge

The next day, Ananya called for another team meeting. This time, she brought with her an activity inspired by Sameer's story.

"We're going to try something different today," she announced. "Each of you will list your strengths on a card, as well as the challenges you face in this project. Then, we'll work together to find ways those strengths and challenges can complement each other."

At first, the team was sceptical. But as they began to share, the room gradually came alive with conversation.

"I'm great with analytics but struggle with presenting ideas clearly," said one teammate.

"I'm the opposite," another chimed in. "I can simplify complex ideas but need help with the data side of things."

By the end of the session, they had mapped out a network of interdependencies—a web where each person's strengths supported someone else's challenges.

Building the Web

Over the next few weeks, Ananya watched her team transform. The silos began to dissolve as people leaned into their interconnected roles. Challenges were no longer individual burdens; they became shared opportunities for growth.

She also noticed something unexpected: collaboration didn't just improve the project; it strengthened the team's morale. There was a newfound sense of camaraderie and mutual respect that had been missing before.

Lessons from the Palace

Ananya reflected on Sameer's story of the Pandavas' palace. The success of the palace wasn't just about skill; it was about trust. Each Pandavas trusted the others to excel in their roles, knowing that the whole was greater than the sum of its parts.

She saw a parallel in her own team. By fostering trust and collaboration, they were building something far more enduring than the project itself—they were building a foundation for future success.

A Conversation with Sameer

Over coffee one evening, Ananya shared her observations with Sameer.

"It's incredible," she said. "Once the team started seeing each other as allies rather than competitors, everything changed. It's like we're finally working as one."

Sameer smiled. "That's the magic of collaboration, Ananya. It's not just about dividing tasks; it's about weaving together strengths and creating a collective momentum. Just like the Pandavas, you've built a palace—not of stone, but of trust and purpose."

As Ananya walked home that night, she thought about the web her team had built. It wasn't perfect, but it was strong—and it was theirs.

She realized that collaboration wasn't just a means to an end; it was an end in itself. It was the art of balancing individuality with unity, creating something far greater than what any one person could achieve alone.

CHAPTER TEN

THE MIRROR OF CHOICES

qThe rain tapped softly against the window as Ananya sat in her office, a stack of reports spread across her desk. The project was progressing, but decisions needed to be made—big ones. Each choice seemed to ripple with uncertainty, and the fear of making the wrong move weighed heavily on her.

Her phone buzzed. It was a message from Sameer:

"When in doubt, look into the mirror. The answers lie within."

Ananya frowned. Was he suggesting self-reflection, or was this just another of his cryptic riddles? Either way, she decided to call him.

The Choice Conundrum

"You've got to help me, Sameer," Ananya began, skipping pleasantries. "I have three options for the next phase of the project, and I can't decide. Each one has risks and potential rewards, but none feel like the obvious answer."

Sameer chuckled on the other end of the line. "Ah, the paradox of choice. Let me tell you a story."

The Mythological Parallel

Sameer began recounting a tale from the Mahabharata.

"Do you remember the moment when Arjuna hesitated on the battlefield of Kurukshetra?" he asked.

"Of course," Ananya replied. "That's when Lord Krishna delivered the Bhagavad Gita."

"Exactly," Sameer said. "But do you know why Arjuna hesitated? It wasn't just fear or confusion—it was a deep inner conflict between his duty as a warrior and his love for his family. He was torn between dharma and emotion, and the choices before him seemed equally unbearable."

"So, what did Krishna do?" Ananya asked, even though she knew the answer.

"He held up a mirror, figuratively speaking. He helped Arjuna see beyond the immediate choices and focus on his higher purpose. Krishna didn't tell Arjuna what to do; he guided him to find his own answer by aligning his actions with his values."

Reflection in Practice

Sameer's words stayed with Ananya long after their conversation ended. That night, she decided to try her own form of self-reflection.

She wrote down the three options for the project, listing their pros and cons. Then, instead of analysing them further, she asked herself a different question:
Which choice aligns most with the vision we set out to achieve?

It was a subtle shift, but it brought clarity. One option, while riskier, felt truer to the project's intentions.

The next day, Ananya presented her decision to the team. As she spoke, she felt a renewed sense of conviction. The choice wasn't without challenges, but it was grounded in purpose—and that made all the difference.

The Ripple Effect

As the project moved forward, Ananya noticed something remarkable. The team, inspired by her clarity, began approaching their own decisions with the same level of introspection. They weren't just asking what to do; they were asking why.

The change was subtle at first but soon became a defining trait of their work culture. Meetings were more focused, conflicts were resolved more thoughtfully, and their collective progress accelerated.

The Mentor's Wisdom

One evening, over tea, Sameer checked in with Ananya.
"How are things going?" he asked.

"Better than I expected," Ananya admitted. "But I realized something: the hardest part of making decisions isn't choosing between options—it's confronting the doubts within yourself."

Sameer nodded. "That's the mirror, Ananya. It doesn't just show you the path; it shows you who you are. And when you align your choices with your values, you not only move forward—you grow."

Later that night, as the rain continued to fall, Ananya wrote in her journal:

"Choices are not just forks in the road; they are reflections of who we are and what we stand for. To choose wisely, we must first understand ourselves."

She closed the journal and smiled. For the first time in weeks, the weight on her shoulders felt lighter—not because the challenges had disappeared, but because she had found clarity in the mirror of her intentions.

CHAPTER ELEVEN

THE SHADOW OF INTENT

Ananya stood on the balcony of her office building, staring at the sprawling city below. The day had been relentless, filled with heated debates about a proposal that had divided her team. The proposal had potential but carried risks that could backfire, putting the company's reputation on the line.

The argument wasn't about the work itself—it was about intent. Could a decision made with the best intentions still lead to harm?

Her thoughts were interrupted by a call from Sameer.

"You sound tired," he said as soon as she answered.

"Exhausted," Ananya admitted. "We're stuck. The team can't agree on whether to move forward with an idea that's risky but well-intended. I keep wondering—is it enough to have the right intent if the outcome could be disastrous?"

The Mythological Parallel

Sameer listened and then offered a story Ananya hadn't heard before.

"Have you ever come across the story of Ashwatthama from the Mahabharata?" he asked.

Ananya shook her head. "I know he was Dronacharya's son, but not much else."

"Ashwatthama was a brave warrior, but his story is one of tragic consequences," Sameer began.

"During the Kurukshetra war, after Dronacharya was killed, Ashwatthama was consumed by grief and rage. Seeking vengeance, he invoked the Brahmastra—a weapon of unimaginable power. But the consequences were devastating. His intent was to end the war by eliminating his enemies, yet his actions led to immense suffering, including the death of unborn children."

Ananya winced. "That's horrific."

"It is," Sameer agreed.

"But here's the lesson: Ashwatthama's intent wasn't evil. He sought justice for his father's death. Yet his inability to consider the broader impact of his actions turned his intent into destruction."

He paused before continuing. "Intent matters, Ananya. But so does foresight. A good intention doesn't absolve us of the responsibility to think through the consequences."

The Corporate Parallel

The next day, Ananya called for a meeting with her team. She shared Ashwatthama's story, drawing parallels to their own dilemma.

"We're not Ashwatthama," she said, "but our situation is similar in one way. We have good intentions, but we need to ensure that our actions don't create unintended harm."

The team spent the day rigorously analysing the proposal, not just for its potential benefits but for its risks. They brainstormed mitigation strategies, tested assumptions, and sought external perspectives.

By the end of the day, they reached a consensus: the proposal would move forward, but with clear safeguards in place to minimize potential fallout.

The Pursuit of Power

As the meeting ended, one of Ananya's colleagues brought up another concern.

"Do you think we're being too cautious?" he asked. "Sometimes it feels like we're holding back because we're afraid of taking risks."

Ananya thought for a moment before answering. "Caution isn't the enemy of progress," she said. "But we have to ask ourselves—are we chasing power for its own sake, or are we pursuing something meaningful?"

Her mind drifted to another story Sameer had once shared, about Ravana from the Ramayana.

"Ravana was one of the most powerful kings of his time," she explained to her colleague. "He had immense knowledge and strength, but his unrelenting pursuit of power blinded him. His desire to prove his dominance led to his downfall."

She continued, "Power isn't inherently bad, but the why behind it matters. Are we using it to create value, or are we just feeding our egos?"

Ananya's Reflection

That evening, as Ananya walked home, she replayed the day's events in her mind. The balance between intent and consequence, between ambition and responsibility, was delicate but essential.

She thought about Ashwatthama and Ravana—two figures with immense potential, brought down by their inability to temper their actions with wisdom.

Ananya resolved to carry these lessons forward, both in her leadership and in her life. She knew that intent would always be her starting point, but clarity, foresight, and accountability would guide her path.

Ananya wrote in her journal that night:

"The right intent is only the beginning. True leadership lies in aligning intent with wisdom, foresight, and responsibility. Without these, even the noblest actions can cast a shadow."

THE FRAGILE CROWN

The city buzzed with excitement as Ananya stepped into the auditorium. She had been invited to a leadership forum to share insights from her journey, but her mind was preoccupied. The theme of the forum—"The Price of Power"—had triggered a wave of questions.

What was power, really? Was it control, influence, or simply the ability to make decisions? And more importantly, was it worth the cost?

The Mythological Parallel

That evening, as she prepared her speech, Ananya called Sameer.

"The forum's theme has me thinking about power," she said. "It's such a complex topic. I want to address it in a way that resonates with people, but I'm struggling to find the right narrative."

Sameer, as always, had a story.

"Have you heard of King Nahusha?" he asked.

Ananya frowned. "The name sounds familiar, but I can't recall the details."

"Nahusha was a great king, known for his wisdom and virtue," Sameer began. "But his story took a dark turn when he was chosen to temporarily take Indra's place as the ruler of the heavens."

"Wait," Ananya interrupted, "a mortal became the king of gods?"

"Yes," Sameer said. "And at first, Nahusha ruled with fairness. But the immense power he wielded began to corrupt him. He grew arrogant and oppressive, even ordering the sages to carry him in a palanquin. When one of the sages stumbled, Nahusha lashed out, kicking him. The sage cursed him, turning him into a serpent."

Ananya was silent, processing the tale.

"Power is fragile, Ananya," Sameer said gently. "It's not just about acquiring it; it's about wielding it with humility and restraint. Lose sight of that, and power will consume you."

The Corporate Parallel

Ananya carried Nahusha's story into her speech at the forum.

"Leadership and power are often seen as synonymous," she began. "But history and mythology teach us that power, without purpose and humility, can be a trap."

She shared Nahusha's story, drawing parallels to modern leadership. "In organizations, power can take many forms—authority, influence, even expertise. But the question we must ask ourselves is: how are we using it?"

Ananya then recounted her own experiences. "There were times when I let my position dictate my actions rather than my principles. I learned the hard way that power isn't about control; it's about responsibility. It's about lifting others, not yourself."

Her words struck a chord with the audience. The Q&A session that followed was filled with introspective questions about balancing ambition with accountability.

The Cost of Power

Later that evening, Ananya reflected on her own relationship with power.

She thought about her early career when she had equated success with climbing the corporate ladder. Power had seemed like the ultimate goal—a measure of her worth. But as she grew, she realized that power, when misused or misunderstood, could isolate, and distort.

She also thought about her team and how her leadership style had evolved. By empowering others, she had found more fulfilment than she ever had chasing individual accolades.

Over coffee the next day, Ananya shared her thoughts with Sameer.

"You were right," she said. "Power is fragile. But it's also transformative when used wisely. It's not about the crown; it's about what you do with it."

Sameer smiled. "Exactly. True power isn't about being the loudest voice in the room. It's about being the one who listens, who uplifts, and who creates space for others to thrive."

He leaned back in his chair. "Remember, Ananya, the crown is only as strong as the head that wears it. Keep your purpose clear, and your power will always serve the greater good."

Ananya penned this in her journal that night:

"Power is not the destination; it is a tool. Its true value lies not in possession but in how it is wielded—with wisdom, humility, and purpose."

As she closed her journal, she felt a renewed sense of clarity. Leadership wasn't about standing above others; it was about standing beside them, guiding, and growing together.

CHAPTER THIRTEEN

THE WEIGHT OF PROMISES

The sun filtered through the blinds as Ananya sat in a strategy meeting, trying to focus. The discussion revolved around a crucial partnership the company was negotiating, but her mind kept drifting to the promises she had made—both to her team and to herself.

Promises were powerful. They built trust, inspired hope, and fostered collaboration. But what happened when circumstances made them difficult to keep?

The Mythological Parallel

Later that day, she met with Sameer to seek his guidance.

"Sameer," she began, "I'm torn. There are commitments I made that now seem impossible to fulfil without compromising something else. How do you decide which promises to honour when the stakes are high?"

Sameer took a sip of his tea, then replied, "Have you heard the story of Karna's vow to Duryodhana?"

Ananya shook her head.

"Karna, born to Kunti but raised by a charioteer, was a complex figure in the Mahabharata," Sameer explained. "He was a great warrior and a man of extraordinary loyalty. When Duryodhana, the Kauravas prince, befriended him and made him a king, Karna vowed unwavering loyalty to him, even knowing Duryodhana's intentions weren't always just."

Sameer continued, "This promises bound Karna to a path that led to his downfall. Even when he discovered his true lineage—that he was the eldest Pandava and rightful heir to the throne—he chose to honour his vow to Duryodhana, fighting against his own brothers in the war."

"Wasn't that...tragic?" Ananya asked, her voice soft.

"It was," Sameer agreed. "Karna's loyalty was admirable, but it came at a great cost—to himself and to others. His story teaches us that not all promises are equal. Honouring a promise should align with dharma—one's sense of right and duty. When a vow conflicts with what is just and beneficial, it must be reevaluated."

The Corporate Parallel

Ananya reflected on Sameer's words during her next team meeting. She decided to address the challenges openly.

"I want to talk about the commitments we've made," she began. "Circumstances have changed, and some of these promises may no longer serve our goals—or the people we made them to."

She outlined the reasons for reconsidering certain commitments, ensuring her team understood the thought process behind each decision.

"It's not about breaking promises," she explained. "It's about adapting to ensure we remain true to our purpose. A promise should never become a prison."

To her relief, the team responded with understanding and support. They brainstormed solutions that honoured the spirit of their commitments while adjusting to the realities they faced.

The Weight of Leadership

That evening, Ananya found herself thinking about the delicate balance between integrity and pragmatism.

She thought of Karna, burdened by a promise that defined his life and ultimately led to his undoing. She also thought of her own role as a leader, where every decision carried the weight of expectations.

Leadership, she realized, wasn't about always having the right answers. It was about making choices that balanced the immediate needs with long-term impact, even if that meant reevaluating past decisions.
Over dinner, Ananya shared her reflections with Sameer.

"You're right," she said. "Not all promises are equal. But isn't there a risk of appearing untrustworthy if we change course?"

"Trust isn't about rigidly sticking to a promise," Sameer replied. "It's about transparency and intent. If people see that you're acting in their best interest and communicating honestly, they'll trust you even when the course changes."

He paused, then added, "Remember, Ananya, leadership is not about being infallible. It's about being accountable."

As Ananya wrote in her journal that night, she captured the essence of her learning:

"A promise is a bridge between intention and action. To honour it is to ensure it leads to the greater good, even if the path must change."

With a clearer perspective, she closed her journal and prepared for the days ahead. The weight of her promises felt lighter—not because the challenges had disappeared, but because she had found a way to carry them with purpose and clarity.

CHAPTER FOURTEEN

A Quiet Departure

The air felt heavy with anticipation as Ananya walked into the café, knowing this would likely be her last conversation with Sameer for a while. The journey they had shared—of questions, reflections, and growth—had been transformative. Yet, she felt a growing sense that this chapter of her life was drawing to a close.

Sameer was already seated by the window, his usual cup of tea in hand. He smiled as she approached, a calm, knowing expression on his face.

The Turning Point

"How are you feeling, Ananya?" he asked, his voice steady but warm.

"I've been reflecting," she began. "On promises, power, and everything we've discussed. It feels like I've reached a turning point—like there's something more waiting for me, but I don't quite know what it is yet."

Sameer nodded. "That's a sign of growth, Ananya. Growth isn't about having all the answers; it's about asking the right questions. And you've started asking some powerful ones."

She looked at him, sensing a shift in his tone. "Sameer...you're speaking as though our conversations are coming to an end."

He chuckled softly. "Not an end, just a transition. My role has always been to guide you to the point where you can guide yourself. And you're there now. The answers you seek won't come from me or anyone else—they'll come from within you."

The Mythological Lesson

Sameer leaned forward, his expression thoughtful. "Do you remember the story of Krishna's departure at the end of the Mahabharata?"

Ananya nodded. "He left the world after guiding the Pandavas through their journey. His departure marked the end of an era, didn't it?"

"Yes," Sameer said. "Krishna's role as a guide was never about dictating actions; it was about empowering the Pandavas to navigate their challenges. Once his purpose was fulfilled, he stepped away, knowing his time with them had served its purpose. His departure wasn't a loss—it was a testament to their growth."

Ananya's eyes widened as the parallel sank in. "You're saying that sometimes a mentor's role is to step away, allowing the person they've guided to walk their path independently."

"Exactly," Sameer said, smiling. "And that's where you are now. You've learned to seek wisdom, to question, and to reflect. The journey ahead is yours to navigate, and I have no doubt you'll do so with grace and strength."

The Final Lesson

Ananya felt a pang of sadness but also a deep sense of gratitude.

"Sameer, if there's one final piece of advice you could give me, what would it be?"

He thought for a moment before replying. "Don't fear the unknown, Ananya. Embrace it. The greatest leaders, the most profound thinkers, and the most fulfilled individuals aren't those who avoid uncertainty—they're the ones who face it with curiosity and courage. Trust your intuition, and let it guide you."

He stood, signalling that their conversation was coming to an end. "Remember, growth isn't linear. There will be setbacks, doubts, and challenges. But each one is an opportunity to learn and evolve. Keep seeking, keep questioning, and keep growing."

The Quiet Departure

As Sameer walked away, Ananya sat quietly, letting his words sink in. She felt a mixture of emotions—gratitude for the wisdom he had shared, a sense of loss at his departure, and an unmistakable excitement for the journey ahead.
She opened her journal and wrote:

"A mentor's greatest gift is the belief they instil in you—the belief that you can find your own path."

Looking out the window, Ananya saw a reflection of herself—not the hesitant, unsure individual she had been months ago, but someone stronger, more introspective, and ready to face the unknown.

As the café emptied and the evening descended, Ananya rose with a quiet determination. Sameer's role in her life might have come to an end, but his lessons would remain with her always.

It was time to embrace the unknown, to explore the deeper truths that lay hidden in both mythology and life itself.

With a renewed sense of purpose, she walked out into the night, ready for whatever lay ahead.

Segment 3 - Bridging the Eternal and the Everyday

"The deeper we dive into the past, the clearer the lens becomes to view the present."

CHAPTER FIFTEEN

THE WEIGHT OF CROWNS

Ananya walked into the dimly lit study, her footsteps echoing against the marble floor. She had been invited to meet someone new—a person her late-night reading group referred to as "The Sage of Realities." The name sounded cryptic, but the recommendation had come from an old colleague she trusted.

As she entered, she noticed an elderly man seated by a wooden desk, his silhouette framed by a shelf full of ancient books. His presence was commanding yet calm, as if he carried the weight of a thousand untold stories.

"You must be Ananya," the man said, rising to greet her. "I'm Vedant." His voice was warm, but there was an undertone of quiet authority.

The Search for Power

After brief introductions, Ananya got straight to the point. "Vedant, I've been reflecting a lot on power—how it's sought, wielded, and often lost. I've seen it destroy relationships and fuel ambitions, but I've also seen it create incredible transformations. I want to understand it better."

Vedant nodded thoughtfully. "Power is a curious thing. It doesn't corrupt as much as it reveals. Would you like to hear a story?"

Ananya smiled. She was already familiar with his method. "Always."

Vedant leaned back in his chair. "Have you heard of King Yayati?"

The name stirred faint memories. "He's the one who... exchanged his old age with his son, isn't he?"

"Exactly," Vedant said. "Yayati was a powerful king, but like many, he wasn't satisfied. Despite having all the wealth and wisdom one could ask for, he was consumed by desire—his yearning for youth, vitality, and pleasure. When the curse of old age was placed upon him, he begged his sons to take his burden so he could continue to enjoy life."

Ananya frowned. "And one of his sons actually agreed to bear the curse, didn't he?"

Vedant nodded. "Yes, his youngest son, Puru, sacrificed his youth for his father. But here's the irony: even after regaining his youth, Yayati realized that desires are insatiable. No matter how much you satisfy them, they only grow. He eventually renounced the world, understanding that true power lies in mastering oneself, not others."

The Modern Reflection

Ananya was silent for a moment, digesting the story. "So, Yayati's pursuit of power—his desire to hold on to youth—was ultimately his downfall?"

"Not his downfall," Vedant corrected. "His lesson. Yayati represents every individual who believes external achievements or possessions will fill an internal void. Power isn't inherently bad, Ananya. But when it's chased for the wrong reasons, it becomes a burden rather than a tool."

She nodded, reflecting on the countless corporate leaders she had encountered who seemed trapped in an endless cycle of chasing titles, influence, or wealth, only to find themselves more unfulfilled than before.

The Personal Challenge

Vedant leaned forward. "Tell me, Ananya—what does power mean to you?"

Caught off guard by the question, she hesitated. "I suppose... it's about influence. The ability to make things happen, to inspire others."

"That's part of it," Vedant said. "But let me offer you a different perspective. Power is also about responsibility—towards others, yes, but also towards yourself. It's about knowing when to step forward and when to step back.

Yayati's story isn't just about desire; it's about accountability. In chasing power, he forgot his role as a father, a king, and a human being."

The words struck a chord. Ananya thought about her own life—the promises she had made, the goals she had pursued, and the sacrifices she had justified along the way. Had she been chasing power without fully understanding its implications?

A New Path

Vedant's voice softened. "There's no shame in ambition, Ananya. But remember this: power is a mirror. It reflects your true self. If you seek it to fill a void, it will magnify that emptiness. But if you use it to serve, to uplift, it becomes a force for good."

She felt a flicker of clarity. "So, the key is balance—knowing when to hold on and when to let go?"

Vedant smiled. "Exactly. And that balance begins with understanding your intentions. Why do you want power? What do you hope to achieve with it? Answer those questions honestly, and you'll find your path."

The Quiet Resolve

As Ananya left the study that evening, her mind was buzzing with thoughts. Vedant's words had opened a door she hadn't even known existed. Power wasn't just about leadership or influence; it was a test of character, a reflection of one's deepest desires and fears.

She wrote in her journal that night:
"The weight of crowns isn't in the metal; it's in the choices of the one who wears it."

Ananya knew her journey was far from over. But with mentors like Vedant and the lessons of mythology guiding her, she felt ready to confront the questions that lay ahead.

SHADOWS OF THE UNSEEN

Ananya arrived at Vedant's study the following week, her thoughts swirling. The story of Yayati had sparked a deeper curiosity—what about those in mythology who made difficult, even questionable choices, but with the right intentions?

Vedant greeted her with his usual calm demeanour, motioning for her to take a seat. This time, a steaming cup of herbal tea awaited her.

"You look restless," Vedant observed.

"I've been thinking about decisions," Ananya admitted. "About how even the best intentions can lead to unintended consequences. Are there stories in mythology where someone acted out of love or duty, but their choices brought pain or chaos?"

Vedant's expression grew serious, the light in his eyes flickering like a flame. "There are many, Ananya. Perhaps none more poignant than the story of Karna."

The Story of Karna

Vedant leaned back, his gaze distant as he began to recount the tale. "Karna was born under extraordinary circumstances, abandoned by his mother Kunti due to societal pressure. Raised by a charioteer, he grew up facing ridicule, yet he harboured a relentless drive to prove himself. Despite his noble heart, Karna's life was a series of complicated choices, each shaped by loyalty, ambition, and the need for acceptance."

Ananya listened intently. "Wasn't Karna known for his generosity?"

"Yes," Vedant replied. "His generosity was unmatched. But it was his loyalty to Duryodhana that defined his destiny. When Duryodhana, an outcast himself, embraced Karna and gave him a kingdom, Karna pledged unwavering allegiance to him—even when he knew Duryodhana was on the wrong path."

"But why would he do that?" Ananya asked, her brows furrowing.

"Because loyalty, for Karna, was more than a virtue. It was his identity," Vedant explained. "He felt indebted to Duryodhana for giving him dignity when the world scorned him. And in his desire to repay that debt, he overlooked his own moral compass."

Reflections on Right and Wrong

Ananya was silent for a moment, absorbing the weight of the story. "So, Karna's loyalty was his strength, but also his downfall?"

Vedant nodded. "Exactly. He teaches us that even the noblest virtues, when taken to extremes, can lead to destruction. His story is a reminder that our choices must balance intent with discernment."

She leaned forward, her voice quieter. "But isn't that unfair? Karna was a good man in many ways. Why should someone with the right intentions suffer so much?"

Vedant's gaze softened. "Because life isn't always fair, Ananya. Mythology doesn't just glorify heroes or villains—it holds a mirror to human complexity. Karna's story shows us that righteousness isn't always rewarded, and mistakes made with the best intentions can still carry consequences."

The Personal Parallel

Vedant shifted his tone. "Now, let's talk about you. Have you ever made a choice that felt right in the moment but led to unforeseen challenges?"

Ananya hesitated, a memory surfacing. "There was a project I led a few years ago," she began. "I pushed hard to secure a deal that I believed would benefit the team and the company. But in doing so, I overlooked how my approach was alienating some of my closest colleagues. I achieved the goal, but I lost their trust."

Vedant nodded knowingly. "And how did that experience shape you?"

"It made me realize that success isn't just about results," Ananya said. "It's about how you achieve them—and who you take along the way."

The Lesson of Shadows

Vedant smiled. "You've just articulated Karna's lesson in your own words. Intent matters, but so does execution.

We must constantly reflect on whether our choices align with our values—not just our goals."

Ananya looked thoughtful. "So, the key is to find a balance between loyalty, ambition, and morality?"

"Yes," Vedant replied. "And to recognize that no one is infallible. What matters is learning from our missteps and striving to do better."

The Weight of Choices

As the conversation wound down, Ananya felt a mix of emotions—gratitude for the insights she was gaining, but also a deeper awareness of the complexities of life and leadership.

That night, she wrote in her journal:
"The shadows of our choices linger long after the moment has passed. To navigate them, we must balance intention with wisdom and courage with humility."

She felt a growing determination to apply these lessons—not just in her professional life but in her personal journey as well.

CHAPTER SEVENTEEN

THE PRICE OF PURSUIT

The air was crisp as Ananya strolled through a lush garden that Vedant had recommended for their next meeting. She found him sitting by a pond, observing the gentle ripples in the water as if reading some hidden wisdom in their dance.

"Nature has a way of teaching us," Vedant said as she approached. "It doesn't rush, yet everything gets accomplished."

Ananya smiled. "Sometimes I wish life worked the same way. But the world we live in is all about speed, competition, and constantly chasing the next big thing."

Vedant gestured for her to sit beside him. "Chasing. That's an interesting word. What do you think happens when someone chases too much?"

"They tire themselves out," she replied. "And sometimes, they lose sight of what they're chasing in the first place."

Vedant's eyes twinkled. "Perfect. That brings us to today's story—of Ravana, the mighty king of Lanka, and his relentless pursuit of power."

The Story of Ravana

"Ravana is often remembered as the villain of the Ramayana," Vedant began. "But few pause to consider the layers of his character. He was an extraordinary scholar, a master musician, and a devout follower of Lord Shiva. His achievements were unparalleled, yet his thirst for power and recognition led to his downfall."

Ananya leaned in. "But what drove him to such extremes? Was it just ego?"

Vedant nodded thoughtfully. "Ego played a significant role, but it was also his inability to find contentment. Ravana's greatness was undeniable, but so was his arrogance. He believed he was invincible, and that belief blinded him to the consequences of his actions—kidnapping Sita being the most infamous of them."

The Thin Line Between Ambition and Arrogance

Ananya frowned. "It's interesting, though. Ambition can drive people to achieve incredible things. Where do you think Ravana crossed the line?"

"Ambition is like fire," Vedant explained. "It can cook your food or burn down your house, depending on how you use it. Ravana's ambition turned destructive because it was rooted in proving his superiority rather than serving a higher purpose."

He paused before adding, "His obsession with power was so consuming that he ignored his dharma—his responsibilities as a king, a brother, and a man of wisdom. That's the lesson he leaves behind: unchecked ambition leads to isolation and eventual ruin."

The Modern Reflection

Ananya thought of the corporate leaders she had admired and the ones she had avoided. "I've seen this happen in organizations too," she said. "Leaders who prioritize their own image over their team's well-being often lose the loyalty of their people. They might achieve short-term success, but it rarely lasts."

Vedant smiled. "Exactly. True power lies in uplifting others, not in asserting dominance. Ravana could have been remembered as one of the greatest kings, but his inability to balance ambition with humility sealed his fate."

The Personal Parallel

Vedant turned the conversation inward. "What about you, Ananya? Have you ever chased something so fiercely that you lost sight of everything else?"

She hesitated. "Yes," she admitted. "Early in my career, I was so focused on proving myself that I pushed people away—friends, colleagues, even family. It took me years to rebuild those relationships."

"And what did you learn from that experience?" Vedant asked gently.

"That no achievement is worth losing the people who matter," she said quietly. "Ambition is important, but it shouldn't come at the cost of humanity."

The Lesson of Contentment

Vedant nodded approvingly. "Ravana teaches us that the price of unchecked ambition is often higher than we realize. It's not about suppressing your drive but about channelling it in ways that align with your values and responsibilities."

Ananya reflected on his words, feeling a mix of gratitude and resolve. "So, the key is to pursue without being consumed—to aim high but stay grounded."

"Precisely," Vedant said. "And to remember that true greatness isn't measured by what you take, but by what you give."

The Quiet Epiphany

That evening, as Ananya walked back through the garden, she felt lighter somehow—as if a burden she hadn't realized she was carrying had been lifted.

In her journal, she wrote:
"Ambition without purpose is a race with no finish line. To truly succeed, we must balance the hunger to achieve with the wisdom to pause."

She knew the road ahead would still have its challenges, but the stories and lessons she was gathering were shaping her in ways she hadn't anticipated.

~

CHAPTER EIGHTEEN

THE FORGOTTEN FLAME

Ananya arrived at Vedant's home earlier than usual. She found him seated by a small bronze statue of a woman, her gaze serene yet powerful. The sculpture exuded an aura of quiet dignity, and Ananya felt drawn to it. "Who is she?" Ananya asked, her voice tinged with curiosity.

Vedant glanced at the statue and smiled. "She is Mandodari, the queen of Lanka. A woman of wisdom, grace, and moral courage. Often overshadowed by Ravana's larger-than-life presence, but her story carries profound lessons."

Ananya settled into her chair. "I've heard of Mandodari, but only as Ravana's wife. What's her story?"

The Story of Mandodari

"Mandodari was much more than Ravana's queen," Vedant began. "She was known for her intellect and her unwavering commitment to dharma, even in the face of her husband's misdeeds. Born to the celestial architect Mayasura and an apsara, Mandodari possessed both beauty and wisdom. She was a voice of reason, often cautioning Ravana against his destructive path."

Vedant paused, his tone growing heavier. "She pleaded with Ravana to return Sita to Rama, warning him of the dire consequences of his actions. But Ravana, blinded by arrogance and obsession, dismissed her counsel. Despite her love for him, Mandodari stood firm in her principles, a silent witness to the tragedy that unfolded."

Ananya looked thoughtful. "It must have been painful for her, watching someone she loved spiral into ruin."

"It was," Vedant said softly. "Yet Mandodari's strength lay in her ability to endure without losing her moral compass. She remained a pillar of dignity, even as Lanka burned around her."

The Traits of a Silent Leader

Ananya tilted her head. "What makes her story relevant today? She couldn't stop Ravana, after all."

Vedant smiled faintly. "True, but leadership isn't always about controlling outcomes. Sometimes, it's about standing firm in your values, even when the odds are against you. Mandodari exemplifies silent leadership—the kind that doesn't seek the spotlight but influences through integrity and resilience."

He added, "Her story teaches us that true strength isn't loud. It's steady, enduring, and often goes unnoticed. But it leaves an indelible mark."

The Modern Parallel

Ananya reflected on the leaders she had encountered in her own life. "I've seen people like that in organizations," she said. "The ones who don't crave attention but quietly keep everything running smoothly.

They're the glue that holds teams together, even during crises."

Vedant nodded. "Exactly. In a world obsessed with charisma and visibility, Mandodari's story is a reminder that quiet strength is just as powerful—sometimes even more so."

The Personal Parallel

Vedant leaned forward. "Now, tell me, Ananya. Have you ever encountered someone who influenced you profoundly, not through grand gestures but through their quiet presence?"

Ananya smiled. "Yes. My grandmother. She wasn't educated in the formal sense, but she had this innate wisdom and calmness. Whenever there was chaos in the family, she would step in—not by raising her voice, but by simply being there, offering perspective. I didn't realize it then, but she shaped a lot of my values."

Vedant's eyes softened. "And what did you learn from her?"

"To listen more, to judge less," Ananya said. "And to remember that sometimes, just being there for someone is the most powerful thing you can do."

The Lesson of Influence

Vedant leaned back. "Mandodari's legacy isn't in the battles she fought or the victories she won. It's in the quiet strength she displayed, the values she upheld, and the dignity with which she navigated her challenges. That's her contribution—and it's no less significant than any warrior's."

Ananya felt a sense of awe. "So, influence isn't about being the loudest voice in the room. It's about the values you embody and the impact you leave behind."

"Precisely," Vedant said. "And that's a lesson worth remembering, both in our personal and professional lives."

The Quiet Resolve

As Ananya left Vedant's home that evening, she couldn't help but think of her own life. How often had she dismissed the quieter voices around her, mistaking silence for weakness?

In her journal, she wrote:
"The greatest leaders often go unnoticed. Their strength lies not in their volume but in their values, not in their commands but in their quiet conviction."

She resolved to listen more, to seek out the unsung heroes in her life, and to honour the lessons they offered.

CHAPTER NINETEEN

THE SILENT WITNESS

The wind carried a faint chill as Ananya walked through the forest trail where Vedant had invited her for a discussion. A secluded wooden bench sat under an ancient banyan tree, its roots weaving stories of their own. Vedant was already seated, a thoughtful expression etched on his face.

"What's today's lesson?" Ananya asked, settling beside him.

Vedant gestured toward the forest. "Tell me, Ananya, do you notice the trees? How they silently stand, witnessing everything without interference?"

Ananya glanced around. "I suppose I do. But what does that have to do with us?"

Vedant smiled. "It reminds me of a story—a story about Vidura, the silent witness of the Mahabharata."

The Story of Vidura

Vedant began, his voice steady yet filled with reverence. "Vidura, the son of a sage and a maidservant, was a man of unparalleled wisdom and integrity.

Born into the Kuru dynasty but barred from kingship because of his lineage, he served as an advisor to the throne."

"Vidura was a master strategist and a beacon of dharma. He was often the lone voice of reason amidst the chaos of Hastinapura, warning against the disastrous actions of Duryodhana and his allies. But, like the trees in this forest, he could only witness the unfolding events, powerless to change the course of history."

The Burden of Powerlessness

Ananya frowned. "It must have been frustrating, knowing the right path but being unable to act."

"It was," Vedant agreed. "Vidura's life was a paradox. He had immense knowledge and influence, yet his advice was often ignored. He warned Dhritarashtra against favouring Duryodhana, urged peace between the Pandavas and Kauravas, and foresaw the calamities to come. But his words fell on deaf ears."

"Why didn't he do more?" Ananya asked.

Vedant sighed. "Sometimes, the constraints of one's role limit their actions. Vidura's duty was to counsel, not to rule. He remained a silent witness because he understood that interfering beyond his role would disrupt the order he sought to preserve."

The Modern Parallel

Ananya reflected on this. "It reminds me of middle managers in organizations. They often have the wisdom to see what's going wrong, but their hands are tied by bureaucracy or politics."

Vedant nodded. "Exactly. Vidura's story resonates deeply in the modern world. It's a reminder that wisdom doesn't always translate into power, and influence doesn't guarantee change. But that doesn't diminish its value. Silent witnesses like Vidura serve as moral compasses, even when their warnings go unheeded."

The Personal Parallel

Vedant looked at Ananya. "Have you ever found yourself in a situation where you knew what was right but couldn't act?"

Ananya thought for a moment. "Yes. There have been times when I've seen friends or colleagues make decisions I knew would lead to trouble. I tried to advise them, but they didn't listen. It's a helpless feeling."

Vedant's gaze softened. "And what did you learn from those experiences?"

"That sometimes, all you can do is speak your truth and let others make their choices," Ananya said. "It's not easy, but you can't force someone to see what they're not ready to see."

The Lesson of Perspective

Vedant leaned back against the bench. "Vidura teaches us the value of perspective. Even when his advice was ignored, he remained steadfast in his principles. He understood that his role wasn't to control outcomes but to offer guidance, planting seeds of wisdom that might bear fruit later."

Ananya nodded. "So, the lesson is to focus on doing what's right, even when the impact isn't immediate or visible."

"Exactly," Vedant said. "Because in the end, the silent witnesses often become the ones who shape history—not through action, but through their enduring values."

The Quiet Resolve

As Ananya walked back home, the story of Vidura lingered in her mind. She felt a newfound respect for the silent witnesses in her own life—those who had offered guidance without expectation, who had spoken their truth without imposing it. In her journal, she wrote:

"The wisest voices are often the quietest. They don't seek to control but to guide, planting seeds of truth that grow in their own time."

CHAPTER TWENTY

THE TURNING POINT

The morning was crisp and clear, the kind that carried an air of renewal. Ananya stood at the base of a hill, where Vedant had asked her to meet for what he called "one last climb together." She looked up, unsure whether he meant it literally or metaphorically, but the glint in his eyes when she arrived told her it was both.

"Ready to climb?" Vedant asked, handing her a walking stick.

"Always," Ananya replied, her voice steady but her heart curious.

As they began their ascent, Vedant set a slower pace than usual, allowing space for conversation and reflection.

The Mountain of Growth

Vedant gestured toward the winding trail ahead. "Life is like this climb, Ananya. Sometimes steep, sometimes gentle, but always moving upward if you're willing to walk."

Ananya smiled. "And sometimes, it feels like you're going in circles."

Vedant laughed. "True. But even the switchbacks serve a purpose—they give you perspective. As you climb higher, the view becomes clearer."

They walked in silence for a while, the sound of crunching leaves underfoot filling the gaps. Finally, Vedant broke the quiet. "Tell me, what has this journey taught you so far?"

Ananya's Reflection

Ananya took a deep breath, collecting her thoughts. "It's taught me that wisdom isn't about knowing all the answers but about asking the right questions. That myths are more than stories—they're mirrors. And that growth isn't about perfection; it's about persistence."

Vedant nodded, his expression one of quiet pride. "And what about your choices? How do you see them now?"

"They're clearer," she said. "I've learned to own them, even the mistakes. I used to think of choices as right or wrong, but now I see them as lessons. Each one shapes me in some way."

Vedant stopped walking and turned to face her. "Exactly. The key isn't avoiding mistakes but learning from them. Growth is about becoming, not arriving."

The Myth of Savitri: A Testament to Resolve

As they rested on a flat rock overlooking the valley, Vedant began to tell a story.

"Do you know the tale of Savitri?" he asked.

Ananya shook her head.

"Savitri was a princess of unmatched intelligence and beauty," Vedant began. "She fell in love with Satyavan, a man fated to die within a year. Despite knowing this, she married him, determined to rewrite his destiny. When Yama, the god of death, came to claim Satyavan, Savitri followed him, refusing to give up."

"How did she manage that?" Ananya asked, intrigued.

"Through wisdom, resolve, and persuasion," Vedant explained. "Savitri's arguments were so compelling that Yama eventually relented and returned her husband's life. But her victory wasn't just about eloquence—it was about her unwavering commitment to what she believed in."

The Strength of Inner Resolve

Vedant turned to Ananya. "Savitri teaches us that strength isn't about force; it's about resolve. She didn't fight Yama with weapons but with words, with unshakeable faith in her purpose."

Ananya leaned back, processing the story. "So, it's about knowing your purpose and staying true to it, no matter how impossible it seems?"

"Exactly," Vedant said. "Life will test you. There will be moments when everything seems stacked against you. In those times, your inner resolve will be your greatest ally."

Ananya's Quiet Transformation

As they resumed their climb, Ananya felt a shift within her. She realized that the lessons she had learned from Vedant and the stories he had shared were no longer just abstract ideas. They had become part of her, shaping how she saw herself and the world.

When they reached the summit, Vedant turned to her with a rare seriousness. "Ananya, this is where I leave you."

She looked at him, startled. "What do you mean?"

"You've grown beyond the need for my guidance," Vedant said gently. "The answers you seek are within you now. My role was to guide you to this point. The next steps are yours to take."

A New Horizon

As Vedant walked away, leaving her at the summit, Ananya felt a mixture of loss and liberation. The view before her was breathtaking, but it wasn't the scenery that captured her attention—it was the sense of possibility.

For the first time, she felt ready to face the world on her own terms, armed with the wisdom she had gathered along the way.

In her journal that evening, she wrote:
"True mentors don't just teach—they set you free. They show you the horizon and trust you to find your way to it."

CHAPTER TWENTY-ONE

FOUNDATIONS OF WISDOM

Ananya stood at the edge of the cliff, the vast expanse of the valley stretching before her. The cool wind brushed against her face, carrying with it the whispers of a thousand untold stories. Vedant had invited her here—not for another lesson, but for what he called a "moment of reckoning."

"I brought you here," Vedant began, his voice steady but soft, "not to teach you something new, but to let you see how far you've come."

Ananya turned to him, her eyes searching. Over the months, Vedant had been her anchor, her guide through the stormy seas of doubt, fear, and confusion. But now, as he spoke, there was an unfamiliar finality in his tone.

"You've walked through myths," he continued, "learned from kings, warriors, sages, and ordinary souls who made extraordinary choices. But the question remains—what have you truly discovered?"

Ananya hesitated, her thoughts racing. She had absorbed lessons on humility, strength, intent, and the pursuit of truth. She had seen herself mirrored in mythological tales, finding clarity in their timeless wisdom. But what had she truly discovered?

"Life is a paradox," she said finally, her voice steady. "Each lesson feels complete until life presents a new challenge. And each challenge redefines what I thought I knew."

Vedant smiled, his eyes gleaming with pride. "Exactly. Wisdom is not a destination, Ananya. It's a continuum—a journey of questioning, reflecting, and growing."

He stepped closer, gesturing to the valley below. "This view—vast, limitless—symbolizes life itself. It's beautiful and overwhelming, but it only reveals its secrets when you embrace its vastness without fear."

Ananya closed her eyes, letting the moment sink in. She could feel the weight of her journey—not as a burden, but as a foundation. Each mythological tale she had encountered, each mentor she had learned from, had left an indelible mark. Yet, standing here, she realized that the journey had always been hers to own.

"Vedant," she began, her voice tinged with emotion, "you've been more than a guide. You've shown me how to see the world differently, to see myself differently."

Vedant shook his head gently. "No, Ananya. I only held up the mirror. You found the courage to look into it. And now, you must carry this wisdom forward—not as a follower, but as a leader."

The words hung in the air, heavy with meaning. Ananya felt a surge of resolve rising within her. She was no longer the hesitant seeker who had stumbled into this journey. She was evolving—stronger, wiser, and ready to step into her own power.

As they stood in silence, Ananya spoke again, this time with clarity. "If wisdom is a continuum, then I know my journey doesn't end here. It begins anew, with each step I take."

Vedant nodded, his expression one of quiet approval. "And so it does. Remember, the greatest lessons are not the ones you are taught, but the ones you discover."

With that, he placed a hand on her shoulder, a gesture of both farewell and encouragement. "It's time for you to walk your path, Ananya. And when you do, remember the myths. They are not just stories of the past—they are the truths of today and the hope of tomorrow."

As Ananya descended the cliff, she felt an unfamiliar lightness in her step. The journey with Vedant had reached its natural conclusion, but her own journey was just beginning. The myths she had explored were no longer ancient tales—they were living, breathing lessons, guiding her in ways she had yet to fully comprehend.

The wind carried her thoughts forward, whispering promises of new challenges, new mentors, and new revelations.

She welcomed them all, knowing that each step would deepen her understanding of the world and of herself with a single thought as —

"The path to wisdom is endless, but every step makes it worth the walk."

CHAPTER TWENTY-TWO

THE PRISM OF POWER

Ananya sat in a bustling café, the aroma of freshly brewed coffee mingling with the hum of lively chatter. Across the table sat a woman she had never met before but whose presence exuded a calm authority. Her name was Tara, a leadership coach with a reputation for helping people uncover their inner strengths. Vedant had introduced them before departing, suggesting that Tara could provide perspectives Ananya might need in the next phase of her journey.

"You've come a long way," Tara began, her tone warm but probing. "But I hear you're still searching for something. Tell me—how do you see power?"

The question caught Ananya off guard. She had never thought about power as a concept, let alone how it might relate to her journey. Still, her curiosity was piqued.

"What do you mean by power?" she asked cautiously.

Tara smiled, as though she had anticipated the question. "Power is not just about control or authority. It's about influence, intent, and impact.

And it's more fragile than most people think. Let me tell you a story."

The Story of Nahusha

"There was once a mortal king named Nahusha, known for his wisdom and virtue," Tara began. "When Indra, the king of the heavens, went into hiding, the gods needed a temporary ruler. They chose Nahusha, elevating him to divine status.

"At first, Nahusha ruled with humility, earning the respect of all. But the intoxicating nature of power soon clouded his judgment. He demanded that the great sages carry him in a palanquin, treating them as mere servants. When Sage Agastya refused, Nahusha insulted him in anger. The sage, in turn, cursed Nahusha, condemning him to live as a serpent on earth.

"The lesson is clear," Tara said. "Power amplifies your intent. When driven by ego, it becomes destructive. But when guided by humility, it can transform the world."

As Ananya absorbed the story, she couldn't help but draw parallels with her own life. Nahusha's tale mirrored so many modern struggles—the lure of success, the ego it inflates, and the fall that inevitably follows when humility is lost.

"So, power itself isn't good or bad," Ananya reflected aloud. "It's the person who wields it—and their intent—that makes the difference."

Tara nodded. "Exactly. And that's where the real challenge lies. Why do you seek power? What do you intend to do with it?"

The Triangle of Power

Tara pulled out a notebook and sketched a triangle on the page, labelling its three points: Intent, Action, and Impact.

"Power flows through these three elements," she explained. "Intent is the why. Action is the how. Impact is the what. Misalign any one of them, and power turns corrosive. Keep them aligned, and it becomes a force for good."

Ananya studied the diagram, feeling its weight. Tara's words echoed the myths she had studied—the stories of Ravana, Duryodhana, and now Nahusha. In each case, intent had defined the outcome, for better or worse.

"What about people who never seek power?" Ananya asked.

"Ah, but even avoiding power is a form of power," Tara replied. "It's a choice, and every choice has consequences. The question is not whether you have power—it's how you choose to use it."

A Paradox to Embrace

Their conversation deepened as Tara shared examples from her work—leaders who had used their influence for both noble and self-serving purposes. Ananya saw herself in those stories, grappling with questions she hadn't yet dared to ask.

"You see, power is a paradox," Tara said. "The more you chase it for personal gain, the less fulfilled you become. But when you use it to uplift others, it becomes a source of profound meaning."

Ananya thought of Vedant's teachings, Sameer's quiet strength, and her own aspirations. She began to see power not as a goal but as a tool—a means to create, inspire, and grow.

As they left the café, Tara's parting words stayed with her:

"Your journey isn't about avoiding power, Ananya. It's about embracing it responsibly, wielding it wisely, and remembering this—true power lies not in control, but in connection."

CHAPTER TWENTY-THREE

THE RIPPLE EFFECT

The air felt crisp as Ananya walked through a tree-lined park in the heart of the city. It had been days since her conversation with Tara, yet her words still lingered in Ananya's mind: *"True power lies not in control, but in connection."*

As she strolled, lost in thought, her phone buzzed. It was a message from an old friend, Aditya. They hadn't spoken in years, but the tone of his message was urgent:

"Need to talk. It's about my company... and me. Can we meet?"

Later that evening, they met at a quiet spot in a co-working café. Aditya, once full of energy and ambition, looked weary. His start-up, which had initially flourished, was now faltering. His employees had grown distant, his investors impatient.

"I don't get it," Aditya confessed. "I've done everything right—built the business, made tough calls, chased opportunities. But somehow, it's all falling apart."

Ananya listened intently, sensing that Aditya's struggles went beyond mere business strategies.

"Tell me, Aditya," she began gently, "why did you start this company in the first place?"

Aditya paused, caught off guard by the simplicity of the question. "I wanted to solve a problem... and create something meaningful."

"And do you still feel that way?" Ananya pressed.

Aditya hesitated, then admitted, "Honestly, I've been so focused on growing the business and proving myself that I've lost sight of why I started it."

The Tale of Yayati

Ananya smiled faintly. "You remind me of a story," she said. "Have you heard of King Yayati?"

Aditya shook his head.

"Yayati was a wise and prosperous king who ruled his kingdom with fairness and vision. But as he grew older, he became consumed by his desire for youth and pleasure. When his time came to renounce worldly life, he pleaded with his son to exchange his youth for Yayati's old age.

"The son, out of respect, agreed. Yayati regained his youth and indulged in every pleasure he could imagine.

Yet, instead of finding satisfaction, he became even more restless and unfulfilled. Only when he finally accepted the natural cycle of life and let go of his desires did he find peace."

Aditya leaned back, the weight of the story settling in. "So, you're saying I've been chasing something that isn't sustainable?"

Ananya nodded. "Yayati's story isn't just about age—it's about the endless pursuit of more. Sometimes, the harder we chase external goals, the further we drift from our true purpose. Maybe it's time to realign with what really matters to you."

Recalibrating Intent

Their conversation shifted as Ananya guided Aditya to reflect on his leadership.

"When was the last time you truly connected with your team?" she asked.

Aditya frowned. "It's been a while. I've been so focused on targets that I've forgotten the people behind them."

"That's your ripple effect," Ananya explained. "Every leader creates ripples—through their actions, their words, and their values. If your focus is purely on the outcome, the people around you will feel it. But if you lead with purpose and empathy, those ripples can inspire and uplift."

Aditya looked thoughtful. "So, it's not just about my goals. It's about how I make others feel in the process?"

"Exactly," Ananya said. "Your power lies in how you influence others, directly or indirectly. And that influence starts with clarity—clarity of intent and connection."

Building the Foundation

As the evening wore on, Ananya shared practical steps for Aditya to rebuild his foundation:

1. Reconnect with Your Why: "Revisit your original vision. What problem were you solving, and why did it matter?"

2. Engage with Your Team: "Hold an open forum. Listen without judgment. Let them feel heard."
3. Lead with Empathy: "Show vulnerability. It's okay to admit you don't have all the answers. It builds trust."
4. Shift the Focus: "Success isn't just about numbers—it's about the impact you create for those around you."

Aditya scribbled notes, his energy slowly returning. "You know," he said with a smile, "I came here looking for business advice, but I think what I really needed was perspective."

The Ripple Becomes a Wave

As Ananya walked home that night, she reflected on their exchange. She realized that she had unknowingly stepped into the role of a mentor, much like Vedant or Tara had been for her.

It was a humbling thought. She wasn't just learning from others—she was now sharing her own wisdom, creating ripples of her own.

And for the first time, Ananya felt the quiet stirrings of a deeper purpose. Her journey wasn't just about her anymore. It was about the lives she could touch, the minds she could inspire, and the ripples she could set into motion.

CHAPTER TWENTY-FOUR

The Two Lives of Ananya

The early morning light filtered through the tall windows of Ananya's apartment, casting long shadows across her cluttered desk. It was a quiet moment, rare and fleeting. The city below was just beginning to stir, but Ananya's mind was already racing.

Over the past months, her life had been a whirlwind of learning, mentoring, and introspection. On the surface, she was thriving—a beacon of growth and transformation. But beneath the polished exterior lay a different story, one she rarely admitted to anyone, even herself.

The Life She Lived

To the world, Ananya was a picture of success. Colleagues admired her for her ability to distil complex ideas into actionable insights. Her friends often turned to her for advice, seeing her as a source of calm and wisdom.

Yet, there were cracks in the facade.

At work, she often felt like she was performing a carefully curated version of herself that met everyone's expectations but left little room for vulnerability. Her achievements, while fulfilling on some level, often felt hollow.

"What's wrong with me?" she whispered to herself one evening after a particularly exhausting day. "Why does it feel like I'm living someone else's life?"

The Life She Wished For

In her quieter moments, Ananya would dream of a different life—one where she wasn't constantly trying to prove herself, where her worth wasn't tied to her achievements.

She imagined waking up without the weight of others' expectations, spending her days creating, exploring, and connecting without fear of judgment.

But those dreams felt distant, almost indulgent. How could she reconcile them with the life she had built?

The Life She Was Becoming

It was during one of these reflective moments that Ananya thought back to the myths she had learned from Sameer, Vedant, and Tara. One story, in particular, came to mind—one she hadn't fully appreciated until now.

The Tale of Eklavya

Eklavya, a young tribal boy, aspired to be the greatest archer of his time. Denied formal training by Dronacharya, he didn't let rejection deter him. Instead, he created a clay idol of the teacher and practiced diligently, surpassing even the most skilled students.

But Eklavya's dedication came at a cost. When Dronacharya

demanded his thumb as a "guru dakshina" to preserve the supremacy of his favoured pupil, Arjuna, Eklavya gave it without hesitation, sacrificing his potential for a principle he believed in.

Ananya pondered the story's nuances. Was Eklavya a victim of injustice, or was he a hero for staying true to his values?

She saw echoes of her own struggles in his journey—the desire to excel, the sacrifices made for approval, and the eventual realization that external validation could never define one's worth.

Reconciling the Two Lives

Ananya's thoughts spiralled as she grappled with her own duality. On one hand, she was the ambitious professional, striving for success. On the other, she yearned to embrace her authentic self, free from the constraints of societal expectations.

That evening, she wrote in her journal—a practice she had recently revived:
"Why do I feel like I'm living two lives? Is it because I'm afraid to let go of the version of myself that others admire?

Or is it because I haven't yet discovered the courage to be fully me?"

The act of writing brought clarity. She realized that her journey wasn't about choosing between the two lives. It was about integrating them—bringing her authentic self into her public life while honouring the lessons and experiences that had shaped her.

Bridging the Gap

In the weeks that followed, Ananya began experimenting with small changes. She started sharing her vulnerabilities with those closest to her, admitting her fears and uncertainties. To her surprise, these moments of honesty deepened her connections rather than diminishing her image.

She also revisited her professional goals, questioning whether they aligned with her true values. Slowly but surely, she began to let go of pursuits that no longer resonated with her.

One evening, as she stood on her balcony watching the city lights, she felt a sense of peace she hadn't known in years. The two lives she had been juggling were starting to merge into one—a life that felt both purposeful and authentic.

The Mirror and the Mask

Ananya's reflections led her to a profound realization:

"We all wear masks, but the goal isn't to discard them completely. It's to make sure the mask reflects who we truly are underneath."

She decided to share this insight in a talk she was invited to give at a leadership summit. Her speech, titled "The Mirror and the Mask," resonated deeply with the audience, sparking conversations about authenticity, vulnerability, and the courage to live fully.

As the chapter of her life with Vedant and Sameer drew to a close, Ananya felt a quiet certainty. She wasn't just a student anymore. She was becoming a guide—not because she had all the answers, but because she was finally asking the right questions.

CHAPTER TWENTY-FIVE

THE COACH WITHIN ME

The echoes of laughter and chatter filled the hallways of the retreat centre. Ananya had just concluded a session with a group of young professionals navigating leadership challenges. As she walked toward the garden for some quiet time, her mind lingered on the phrase she had scribbled in her journal earlier that morning:

"The journey of transformation begins when we meet the coach within ourselves."

She paused by a bench, her thoughts drifting back to her own journey. It had been years since she first sought answers from mentors who guided her. But now, as she listened to the questions and doubts of others, she felt a shift—a realization that she was no longer just learning but also guiding, not as an external authority but by encouraging others to find their own path.

A Question of Balance

During the session, a participant named Karan had posed a question. "How do you balance being empathetic toward your team while maintaining authority?"

The room had fallen silent as everyone awaited Ananya's response. For a moment, she hesitated, unsure if she had the perfect answer. Then, a story from the Mahabharata came to mind—one that had often guided her in similar dilemmas.

The Story of Yudhishthira

"Let me tell you about Yudhishthira," Ananya began, her voice calm yet deliberate. "He was the eldest Pandava, known for his unwavering commitment to dharma. But this commitment was often tested.

"One of the most striking moments came during the Rajasuya Yajna, a grand ceremony to establish his authority as emperor. Despite his role as king, Yudhishthira chose to honour Lord Krishna as the chief guest, acknowledging that leadership isn't about claiming the highest seat but recognizing the contributions of others.

"Yet, this same Yudhishthira struggled during the game of dice, where his sense of duty to family and the rules of the game blinded him to the harm his decisions caused. His story teaches us that balance isn't a fixed state—it's a dynamic process of aligning our values with the needs of the moment."

Karan nodded thoughtfully, and others in the group began to share their perspectives, the conversation flowing organically.

Ananya realized that the story hadn't just provided an answer—it had opened a space for introspection and dialogue.

The Coach Within

Later that evening, as Ananya reflected on the day's events, she wrote in her journal:

"The best coach doesn't give answers; they guide you to ask the right questions."

She thought about her own journey, the mentors who had shaped her—Sameer, Vedant, and others. Each of them had guided her not by imposing their wisdom but by helping her uncover her own.

It was then that she recognized the coach within herself. It wasn't about having all the answers or being infallible. It was about listening, sharing stories, and creating a space for others to find their truth.

An Unexpected Encounter

The next day, during a break, Ananya found herself in conversation with Meera, a participant from another group. Meera spoke about her struggles with self-doubt and her tendency to seek validation from others.

"Sometimes I feel like I can't trust my own judgment," Meera admitted.

Ananya smiled knowingly. "You remind me of myself," she said, "or at least the version of me that always sought answers outside myself. But let me tell you something—it's not about finding the perfect mentor or guide. It's about discovering the coach within you."

Meera looked intrigued. "How do I do that?"

"Start by listening to your inner voice," Ananya replied. "Not the one that doubts or criticizes, but the one that asks, 'What truly matters to me?' That's where your journey begins."

A Legacy of Coaching

Over the next few weeks, Ananya continued to notice this shift in herself. She was no longer just a participant in life's lessons; she was actively shaping the experiences of others. But she did so with humility, recognizing that her role wasn't to lead or direct—it was to empower.

One evening, as she prepared for another session, she wrote:

"The coach within isn't a destination—it's a constant dialogue between who we are, who we've been, and who we aspire to be."

With this thought, Ananya stepped into the room, ready to guide others toward their own realizations.

The Journey Ahead

Ananya's journey wasn't over—it had simply evolved. The coach within her wasn't a replacement for the mentors she had learned from but a continuation of their legacy. And now, she was ready to pass that legacy on, one story, one question, and one moment of connection at a time.

CHAPTER TWENTY-SIX

ECHOES OF THE PAST

The light drizzle on the windowpane mirrored the faint unease in Ananya's heart. She sat at her desk, staring at an old notebook that had accompanied her during the early days of her journey. Its pages were filled with hurried notes, reflections, and sketches—artifacts of a time when every answer seemed just out of reach.

Today, however, Ananya wasn't seeking answers for herself. She was looking for stories that could inspire a new group of mentees she had recently taken under her wing. Among the pages, a phrase caught her eye:

"In the pursuit of power, we often lose sight of purpose."

Her mind instantly travelled back to one of her most memorable lessons—stories of kings and warriors whose thirst for power had shaped their fates, for better or worse.

The Allure of Power

During one of her sessions with Vedant, he had shared the tale of Ravana, the demon king of Lanka. "Ravana was a man of immense knowledge," Vedant had explained. "A scholar, a devotee of Lord

Shiva, and a ruler who built one of the most prosperous kingdoms of his time.

Yet, his downfall was triggered by his insatiable desire to prove his superiority."

Vedant's words had lingered with Ananya. Ravana wasn't a one-dimensional villain. His ambition and intellect were unparalleled, but so was his hubris.

"How does one draw the line between ambition and arrogance?" Ananya had asked him.

Vedant had smiled. "By staying rooted in your purpose. Ambition becomes dangerous when it serves only the self and ignores the greater good."

A Test of Leadership

Ananya's current mentees were a diverse group—each grappling with the pressures of modern leadership. One of them, Aarav, was a young entrepreneur who had built a successful business but was struggling to retain his team.

"They say I'm too demanding," Aarav confessed during a one-on-one session. "But isn't that the price of excellence?"

Ananya saw in Aarav a reflection of Ravana—not in his flaws but in his potential. She decided to share the story.

"Ravana demanded excellence too," she began.

"He was so focused on his vision of power that he overlooked the people who could have helped him achieve it. He ruled with fear, not trust, and in the end, even his own brother turned against him."

Aarav looked thoughtful. "So, what should I do differently?"

"Excellence doesn't have to come at the cost of empathy," Ananya said. "Lead with trust, and people will strive to meet your expectations not out of fear but out of respect."

Reflections on Power

Later that evening, Ananya found herself revisiting the stories of other mythological figures who had grappled with the allure of power. From Duryodhana's envy to Indra's insecurity, the narratives were as relevant today as they had been centuries ago.

She pondered the recurring theme: Power, in itself, wasn't the problem. It was how individuals chose to wield it that determined their legacy.

Her own journey, too, had been marked by moments of power—whether in her career or in the influence she held as a mentor. But each time, she had asked herself: "Is this serving my purpose, or just my ego?"

A Lesson Shared

The next day, during a group discussion, Ananya posed a question:

"What does power mean to you?"

The responses varied. Some saw it as influence, others as freedom, and a few as responsibility.

"Power is all of those things," Ananya said, "but it's also fleeting. What truly lasts is how you use it. If your power uplifts others, it becomes a force for good. If it isolates you, it becomes a trap."

The room fell silent as the participants reflected on her words.

A Journey of Balance

As the session ended, Ananya felt a sense of fulfilment. She had shared not just stories but also the wisdom they carried—lessons that had shaped her own path.

Walking back to her office, she thought of Vedant and Sameer, of the myths they had introduced her to, and of the insights she had drawn from them. Now, it was her turn to pass those lessons on, weaving them into the lives of others, one story at a time.

Her journey was far from over, but she felt ready for the next chapter. For now, though, she was content to walk alongside those who were just beginning theirs.

CHAPTER TWENTY-SEVEN

A Mirror to the Self

The crisp morning air carried a sense of renewal as Ananya stood before a group of young leaders at an outdoor retreat. She held a delicate hand mirror, its frame adorned with intricate carvings, a gift from her grandmother. Raising it, she began, "What do you see when you look in a mirror? Is it just a reflection of your appearance, or something deeper?"

The question hung in the air, drawing puzzled expressions and intrigued whispers. She smiled knowingly. Today's session wasn't about answers—it was about questions, the kind that turned a gaze inward.

The Mirror of Draupadi

As the session unfolded, Ananya recounted the story of Draupadi, the queen of the Pandavas. "Draupadi's life was a series of reflections—of her courage, her vulnerability, and her sense of justice," she began.

She described the infamous court scene where Draupadi was humiliated, stripped of her dignity while the elders remained silent.

"In that moment, she held up a mirror not just to her oppressors but to the entire court, forcing them to confront their values—or lack thereof."

Ananya paused, letting the weight of the story settle. "Draupadi didn't just react to her circumstances; she challenged them, using her pain as a catalyst for change. Her story reminds us that sometimes, the mirror we hold up to others is as important as the one we hold to ourselves."

A Personal Reflection

Ananya often thought of Draupadi when faced with her own moments of doubt and frustration. There had been times in her career when she'd felt unheard, moments when she'd questioned her worth.

One such moment stood out vividly—a meeting where her ideas were dismissed until a male colleague presented them as his own. The sting of invisibility had been sharp, but instead of retreating, Ananya had chosen to address it directly.

"May I clarify that this suggestion was mine?" she had said, her tone firm but composed. The room had fallen silent, and her statement had set a precedent for the conversations that followed.

Looking back, she realized that the courage to speak up had come from years of self-reflection and the stories she had internalized—stories like Draupadi's.

The Participants' Mirrors

During the retreat, Ananya invited the participants to share moments when they had faced their own mirrors. One by one, they spoke:

- A young manager admitted to avoiding conflict with a difficult team member, only to realize that her fear was rooted in her own insecurity.
- A startup founder shared how his obsession with perfection had led to burnout, not just for himself but for his entire team.
- A teacher reflected on how her frustration with her students often mirrored her own unfulfilled dreams.

Each story revealed a layer of vulnerability, and with it, a shared humanity. Ananya listened intently, guiding the discussion with gentle prompts but allowing the participants to find their own insights.

The Mirror Within

Later that evening, as the group gathered around a bonfire, Ananya shared one final thought. "The mirror doesn't lie," she said, holding up her grandmother's gift. "But it also doesn't judge. It simply shows you who you are in that moment. The real question is: What will you do with that reflection?"

She passed the mirror around the group, inviting each participant to hold it for a moment. Some looked at it with curiosity, others with hesitation, but each gaze was uniquely personal.

When the mirror returned to her, Ananya held it up to her own face. For the first time in years, she felt no need to change the reflection staring back at her.

A New Chapter

As the retreat ended, Ananya felt a sense of closure—not just for the event but for a chapter in her own life. The journey she had begun as a seeker was now evolving into one of a guide. Yet, she knew the two roles were inseparable; to lead others, she had to continue leading herself.

Packing her belongings, she slipped the mirror into her bag, a reminder of the questions that had brought her here and the answers still waiting to be discovered.

The road ahead was uncertain, but Ananya felt ready to walk it—not with certainty, but with clarity.

CHAPTER TWENTY-EIGHT

THE LIGHT WITHIN

Ananya stood on the threshold of a significant moment, one she never imagined for herself. The gentle evening sun bathed the room in a golden hue, reflecting the quiet but monumental shift that had taken place within her. Over the months, her life had been a whirlwind of lessons, mentors, challenges, and self-discovery. But today, she felt different—not because the world around her had changed, but because she had.

As she sat by her desk, she glanced at her journal, a repository of her thoughts, fears, and epiphanies. Her fingers traced the leather-bound cover as if it held secrets waiting to be unveiled. Vedant's parting words echoed in her mind: "Wisdom is not what you possess; it's what you inspire in others."

For so long, she had sought answers from those around her—Sameer, Rehan, and Vedant—each of them a guiding force in their own way. Yet, Ananya realized that the lessons they had imparted weren't meant to remain theirs. They were hers to internalize, embody, and pass forward.

Tonight was different. Tonight, she was no longer the mentee.

The moment of realization had come during an impromptu conversation at a coffee shop earlier that day. A young colleague,

Arjun, had approached her with hesitation, a tangle of self-doubt evident in his demeanour.

"I'm not sure if I'm doing the right thing, Ananya," he had said, fidgeting with his coffee cup. "I feel like I'm stuck, trying to balance expectations and my own aspirations. It feels impossible to do both."

Ananya had smiled—a soft, knowing smile that came not from a place of superiority, but from empathy. "You know, Arjun," she began, "there's a story I once read about a river and its flow."

Arjun leaned in, curiosity replacing his nervousness.

"There was a river," she continued, "that flowed down from the mountains, cutting through rocks, carving valleys, and nourishing the land. It wasn't always smooth; the river encountered obstacles—boulders, fallen trees, and narrow passages. But it never stopped. Sometimes, it found new paths. Other times, it simply flowed over or around the barriers. Its purpose wasn't to fight the obstacles, but to keep flowing, knowing that its destination wasn't a place, but the journey itself."

Arjun sat in silence, the weight of her words sinking in. "So, you're saying... I don't have to have it all figured out right now?"

"Exactly," Ananya replied. "Life isn't about having all the answers. It's about moving forward, one step at a time, and trusting that the path will reveal itself as you go."

That conversation lingered with Ananya as she reflected on her own journey. She realized that every mentor she had encountered had been like a river, carving paths through her thoughts and beliefs, leaving her stronger and more resilient. And now, it was her turn to be the river for someone else.

As the evening deepened, Ananya picked up her journal and began to write. But this time, her words weren't for herself—they were for those who might one day seek guidance from her.

"Lessons from the Path," she titled the page, before listing the truths she had come to understand:

1. The power of intent: Every action begins with intent. It is the foundation of integrity and authenticity.
2. The strength of vulnerability: Strength isn't about never falling; it's about rising with grace and courage.
3. The importance of balance: True success lies in finding harmony between ambition and contentment.
4. The beauty of imperfection: Growth comes not from being flawless, but from embracing and learning from flaws.

As she wrote, she felt a quiet satisfaction—a sense of fulfilment that came not from what she had achieved, but from what she could now give.

Later that night, Ananya found herself sitting on her balcony, gazing at the stars. For the first time, she felt the weight of her journey lifting, replaced by a sense of purpose.

Her phone buzzed— a message from Arjun. "Thank you for today, Ananya. I feel like I can finally breathe again."

Ananya smiled. It wasn't about being a mentor or a coach, she realized. It was about being present, listening, and guiding others to discover the answers they already carried within.

In that moment, Ananya knew she wasn't just stepping into a new role—she was embracing the essence of what her journey had prepared her for. The journey ahead wasn't just hers; it was a shared path, illuminated by the light she could now help others find within themselves.

CHAPTER TWENTY-NINE

AFTEREFFECTS OF CHANGE

Ananya sat by the large bay window in her new apartment, gazing at the sprawling city skyline. The view, though breathtaking, was overshadowed by a whirlwind of thoughts. The past weeks had been transformative. Vedant's guidance had left a mark, but this phase felt different—she was no longer being mentored. Instead, she was navigating the labyrinth of her life alone, trying to piece together lessons learned from others and from herself.

Her phone buzzed, snapping her out of her thoughts. It was a message from Aarav, a colleague she had recently mentored.

"Thank you, Ananya. Your advice made a difference. I'm presenting the proposal next week. Fingers crossed!"

She smiled. There was a quiet satisfaction in seeing someone flourish because of her words, her guidance. But it also raised a question: Was she stepping into a new role? Could she, who once struggled to find her path, now guide others toward theirs?

Later that day, she found herself in a quaint café, sipping chai. She had planned to read, but the hum of conversations around her was oddly compelling. People talked about careers, relationships, and dreams—fragments of life interwoven with hope and uncertainty.

One voice stood out. A young woman at the next table spoke passionately about being overlooked for a leadership position. Her frustration was palpable. Ananya instinctively leaned in, not to intrude but to understand.

The woman's words echoed her own struggles years ago, when she felt invisible, her potential buried under doubts. Without realizing it, Ananya scribbled a thought in her notebook:

"Leadership isn't about recognition; it's about conviction—*conviction in your values, your vision, and your ability to uplift others.*"

She closed her notebook, feeling a rush of clarity. Her journey wasn't just about personal growth anymore. It was about sharing, mentoring, and creating a ripple effect.

That evening, as she prepared for bed, Ananya revisited a story from the Mahabharata. She remembered the tale of Vidura, the wise counsellor to the Kuru dynasty. Vidura was a man of principle, a silent force of wisdom amidst chaos. He didn't seek power, yet his influence shaped decisions that rippled through history.

Reflecting on Vidura, Ananya saw a parallel to her own journey. Like him, she wasn't in a position of absolute power. Yet, her insights and actions could steer outcomes, even if subtly. The thought was both humbling and empowering.

She jotted another note:

"True leadership is not about being at the forefront but about steering from the shadows with integrity and wisdom."

The following week, Ananya hosted her first informal mentorship session at work. It wasn't a grand affair—just a few colleagues gathered in a conference room, sharing challenges, and discussing solutions.

As the session ended, one of them said, "Thank you, Ananya. You have a way of making things clear, of showing a perspective we hadn't considered."

Walking out of the room, Ananya felt a quiet fulfilment. She realized she didn't need a title or a stage to lead. Her journey had come full circle—from a seeker of wisdom to a silent guide for others.

Her notebook now bore a new title on the last page:
"The Coach Within Me."

Ananya smiled!!

The journey wasn't over, but she knew she was ready for whatever came next.

The echoes of her past had shaped her present, and now, she was becoming the echo for others.

CHAPTER THIRTY

JOURNALS OF THE MIND AND MYTH

"Wisdom often begins with reflection, and reflection often begins with a pen."

Ananya flipped through the pages of her journal, its edges softened with wear. Each entry told a story—not just hers, but the stories of myths that had become her companions. These were not just lessons from ancient tales; they were guideposts that had illuminated her path.

But now, as she stared at the blank page before her, she realized the journal wasn't just about her anymore. It was for everyone who had ever felt the weight of uncertainty, the pull of self-doubt, or the need to find purpose in chaos. She smiled, placed her pen on the paper, and began to write.

Entry 1: Resilience in the Face of Destiny

"When the waves of life pull you under, remember Hanuman—his greatness was realized not in the comfort of knowledge, but in the chaos of forgetfulness."

There was a time when I doubted my abilities, much like Hanuman before he discovered his latent strength. His story reminded me that even the most powerful among us need a nudge to awaken their true potential. It wasn't about finding strength—it was about remembering it was always there.

What I learned: You don't need new wings to fly; you just need the courage to leap.

Entry 2: The Burden of Promises

"Karna teaches us that the weight of our word can either elevate or shackle us—it all depends on the intent behind the promise."

I often wondered if keeping my word always meant doing the right thing. Karna's unwavering loyalty to Duryodhana, despite knowing the consequences, taught me that promises made without introspection can become chains. In leadership and life, intent matters more than obligation.

What I learned: Promises are powerful; wield them wisely.

Entry 3: Leadership Beyond Titles

"Rama didn't lead because he was a prince; he led because he understood the weight of responsibility."

Titles are fleeting, but actions endure. Watching Rama's story unfold made me question my own responsibilities. Was I leading because of my role or because I genuinely cared? Leadership isn't a crown; it's a choice, made every single day.

What I learned: **True leaders earn respect by walking the talk, not by wearing the crown.**

Ananya closed her journal, her mind racing with countless other lessons she could share. But she paused, realizing this wasn't just her journey anymore.

"It can be you," she whispered.

The journal wasn't meant to end with her. It was an invitation for others to reflect, to question, and to find their own lessons in the myths that surrounded them.

You don't have to be Ananya. You could be someone like her. Or perhaps a mentor like Sameer. Or maybe you're both.

The myths don't belong to one person—they belong to anyone willing to listen.

Ananya left her journal open on the desk, the pen resting beside it, inviting the next story to begin.

CHAPTER THIRTY-ONE

A JOURNEY OF GRATITUDE

"Every person we meet, every story we hear, leaves an imprint. The beauty of a journey lies not in its destination but in the connections, we make along the way."

Ananya sat by the window of her small apartment, gazing at the moonlit sky. Her journal lay open before her, its pages filled with reflections, lessons, and moments of transformation. The faint rustle of the trees outside seemed to whisper the echoes of her journey.

Her thoughts wandered to the people who had shaped her path. Sameer, with his gentle wisdom, had taught her to see herself as more than just a seeker—he had shown her the strength in vulnerability. Vedant, with his probing questions and mythological parallels, had challenged her to dig deeper, to embrace the discomfort of self-discovery.

And then there were the stories. The myths. The timeless tales that had once seemed distant but now felt like trusted companions.

Gratitude for the People

Ananya reflected on the mentors who had stood by her, guiding her at every turn.

Their roles in her life had shifted—sometimes they were challengers, sometimes encouragers—but their impact remained profound.

"Sameer taught me to embrace the coach within, and Vedant reminded me to see life as a tapestry of stories," she thought.

But it wasn't just the mentors. Her journey had been enriched by fleeting encounters—friends who had questioned her choices, colleagues who had shared their stories, even strangers whose words had sparked something within her.

"Each person I met was a part of my journey, teaching me something I didn't know I needed to learn," she whispered to herself.

Gratitude for the Lessons

Her journal was filled with the voices of characters from the Mahabharata and Ramayana. They were no longer distant heroes or abstract archetypes.

Draupadi's resilience in the face of injustice had taught Ananya the strength of standing tall, even when the world tries to bring you down.

Arjuna's hesitation and eventual clarity reminded her that doubts are a natural part of decision-making, but action defines who we become.

Even Ravana, the complex antagonist, had shown her the duality of ambition—a force that could inspire or consume.

"I owe so much to these stories," she thought. "They gave me a lens to view my life, to understand my challenges, and to grow beyond them."

Gratitude for the Journey

Ananya turned to the final page of her journal and wrote:
"Thank you."

It was a simple statement, but it carried the weight of her entire journey—gratitude for the myths that had guided her, for the mentors who had walked beside her, and for herself, for continuing to move forward even when the path wasn't clear.

She reflected on how her relationship with mythology had changed. What once felt like distant tales of gods and kings now resonated with her daily life. She saw their truths in her own struggles, their lessons in her own decisions.

"The myths are alive," she thought. "They live in us, in the way we face our challenges, in the way we lead, and in the way we love."

Ananya stood by the window, letting the cool night breeze wash over her. Her journey wasn't over—it never would be. There were still questions to ask, stories to uncover, and lessons to learn.

But tonight, she wasn't searching for answers. She was simply grateful for the journey so far.

As she closed her journal, she made a silent promise:
To carry forward the wisdom she had gained, to honour the myths

by living their lessons, and to guide others as she had been guided.

She smiled, feeling a deep sense of peace. The journey ahead was uncertain, but for the first time, she felt ready to embrace it with an open heart and mind.

The myths had shown her the way. Now, it was her turn to keep walking.

"Gratitude is the bridge between what was and what will be. It is the essence of every journey, every story, and every life."

P.S.

Dear Reader,

As you close these pages, I want to thank you for accompanying me on this journey. What began as a conversation between myths and mindsets has now become a shared experience between us. I trust that, like me, you've found moments of revelation, of introspection, and perhaps even a few questions that will stay with you long after you've read the last word.

The stories we explored together—whether from the Mahabharata, Ramayana, or the lessons embedded in Ananya's life—are not confined to ancient times. They live in the choices we make, in the paths we take, and in the wisdom, we choose to carry forward.

But this isn't the end. It's a new beginning. Just as Ananya's journey of growth continues, so does yours. With every myth you reflect on, and every mindset you choose to shape, you have the power to craft your own story.

Remember, the lessons we've explored are not the final word on leadership, power, or promises. They are an invitation to dig deeper, to reflect more, and to apply these timeless truths to your own life.

So, as you move forward, I encourage you to carry with you not just the ideas shared within these pages, but the curiosity to continue learning, evolving, and leading with wisdom.

Your journey is uniquely yours—don't be afraid to embrace it fully, with all the complexities and contradictions that come with it. You must contemplate upon;

"Life is not a journey of answers but of questions. Myths teach us that within every story lies a reflection of ourselves. The mindsets we choose are the bridges we build between ancient wisdom and modern living. Keep walking, for the story of your life is still being written."

Thank you for allowing me to be a part of your growth. The best is yet to come.

With deep respect and gratitude,
Deepak Sharma